The Alluring

Félicien Champsaur

The Alluring

translated, annotated and introduced by
Brian Stableford

A Black Coat Press Book

ISBN 978-1-61227-909-1. First Printing. December 2019. Published by Black Coat Press, an imprint of Hollywood Comics.com, LLC, P.O. Box 17270, Encino, CA 91416. All rights reserved. Except for review purposes, no part of this book may be reproduced or transmitted in any form or by any means, electronic or mechanical, including photocopying, recording, or by any information storage and retrieval system, without permission in writing from the publisher. The stories and characters depicted in this novel are entirely fictional. Printed in the United States of America.

Introduction

L'Attirante by Félicien Champsaur (1858-1934), here translated as *The Alluring*, was originally published by Ferenczi in 1931; it was the author's last novel, written—or, more precisely, dictated—in his seventy-third year. It is not well-known, and does not, at the time of writing, appear in the list of the author's works appended to his Wikipedia entry, perhaps because of a slight discomfort occasioned by its symbolism. Although it is not very explicit, what the text reveals about the stance of the protagonist's sculpted self-portrait is an adequate explanation of why the references to it are so carefully elliptical. It was by no means the first time that Champsaur had skirted the unmentionable so closely in his works, but the particular unmentionable that he saved for last was to remain taboo in respectable print for a good while longer.

L'Attirante is what is known in English as a Robinsonade—an account of a castaway on a desert island and his hard battle for physical and psychological survival. French literature is particularly rich in such narratives, and they became a particular fascination of the Romantic Movement, to whose ultimate Decadent phase Champsaur was an enthusiastic recruit at the beginning of his colorful career, and which he never fully deserted when he became a best-selling writer continually under pressure to pander to his market. France is however, very hospitable to writers who can attain enormous sales while sticking stubbornly to their eccentricities, jealous of their own uniqueness. Few others, if any, contrived such an idiosyncratic range of subject matter as Champsaur, or exhibited such an adventurous spirit, and it is typical of him that, having decided to write a Robinsonade, aware that he was following in a great tradition, he wanted to make it a Robinsonade that would go further than any other: a kind of ultimate Robinsonade.

Many writers following in the footsteps of Daniel Defoe had complained that the original Robinson Crusoe had been far too generously treated by his author in the matter of supplying him with the apparatus required to live in a quasi-civilized manner on his not-so-desert is-land—a generosity habitually matched by Jules Verne, the most prolific writer of Romantic Robinsonades—and several of those detractors had been enthusiastic to take the fundamental thought-experiment a good deal further in the imaginative investigation of the minimum re-quirements for human physical survival and the mainte-nance of a viable state of mind.

In France, X. B. Saintine (Joseph-Xavier Boniface) had taken a particular interest such matters, presenting a kind of ultimate desert island in "L'Île du cocotier" (1837; tr. as "The Island of the Coconut Palm") and writing an account of a castaway much more closely based on the actual experiences of Alexander Selkirk—the inspiration for Crusoe—than Daniel Defoe's in *Seul* [Alone] (1857). By Champsaur's time, however, a more extravagant exercise in extremism had been produced by the American writer Douglas Frazar in *Perseverance Island; or, The Robinson Crusoe of the Nineteenth Cen-tury* (1888), in which the castaway is delivered to his problematic refuge stark naked with no possessions but two pins and his ingenuity. Champsaur might well have known about the latter volume, since he is careful to deprive his naked castaway even of the two pins, and to hurl him on to the shore of a desert island devoid of the rich vegetation of which Frazar's hero made such prolific use, merely supplying him with a single grove of coconut palms, only four of which have resisted the effects of a recent tempest.

In the later chapters of the novel, Champsaur gradually relents on that scrupulous minimalism, and adopts a more Vernian approach to the serendipity of his hero, eventually permitting him to achieve an improbable comfort, except when his occasional recklessness delivers him into danger of imminent horrible death. That permission of physical ease is, however, a means of concentrating more intently on the other aspect of the problem. The author's principal interest is not in the basic requirements for physical survival but in the subtler demands of mental survival: hypothetical solutions to the problem of psychological isolation. The latter issue is presumably far more relevant to the fundamental appeal of the genre of Robinsonades than the former, since it reflects a common sensation by virtue of which people can feel isolated and lonely even in the midst of a crowded quotidian existence.

In his approach to the problem of coping with isolation and a pathological lack of human contact, Champsaur follows much more closely in the literary footsteps of Saintine than those of Verne, although in other regards he is much more Vernian; he is, for instance, careful to appropriate Verne's perennial fascination with monstrous creatures, as Frazar had also done. Every good castaway requires a symbolic dragon to slay if he is to lay serious claim to heroic status, but Saintine never assumed for a moment that a physical triumph of that sort could provide a durable psychological crutch, and Champsaur subjects the issue to a similar relegation. In so doing, he draws not only on the legacy of *Seul*, but also that of Saintine's classic *Picciola* (1837), which focuses closely on the battle undertaken by a prisoner condemned to lifelong solitary confinement to preserve his sanity. Champsaur, unsurprisingly, makes his hero an artist—a sculptor, in this case—who necessarily turns to his art as his primary recourse against the pressures of loneliness.

Champsaur is acutely aware, however, that the recourse in question is a double-edged sword; as a firm believer in the doctrine that genius is akin to madness, he is not in any doubt that the potential "escape" provided by absorption in artistic creativity is not so much a salvation of sanity as a flight therefrom. An examination of the fundamental nature of art, stripped of all its social associations, is part and parcel of the problem that the author set himself in conceiving the ultimate Robinsonade. He thus makes no bones about equipping his hero from the very start of the narrative with acute emotional problems, which have precipitated a crisis of sorts even before the ship in which he is sailing for France in 1915 is sunk by a German torpedo. In that regard, Jean Harvez is by no means an anomalous Crusoe—many refugees on desert islands find themselves initially relieved of inconvenient baggage left behind—but he is, once again, more extreme than most in his vulnerability to that legacy and to the threat of not merely being overtaken by it but overwhelmed.

That, in essence, is the real story of *L'Attirante*, and of the alluring in question, and one of the most intriguing things about the narrative is the remarkable understatement of that aspect of the hero's problem, about which the narrative only provides subtle hints. As a

Symbolist—and he began his literary career in the 1880s, in close association with the birth of the Symbolist and Decadent movements—Champsaur had always seemed rather garish in his imagery, and *L'Attirante* is not exempt from a certain brutality in its representation of the crucial image of the masterpiece that Harvez is led to recreate, but that brutality is combined with a deliberate imprecision regarding the sequence of events attendant upon the creation of the original statue, which left the sculptor so distressed that he had to flee from Paris to Brazil. About the model for the statue and her interaction with the sculptor we are told nothing at all, except for the curious triple echo of her nickname, the significance of which is left almost entirely to the reader's imagination: a puzzle whose insolubility provides the story with a core of mystery that reaches far beyond the superficial depictions of the narrative.

It cannot be said that *L'Attirante* is one of Champsaur's best-written books. It shows many of the symptoms of books dictated to an amanuensis—or amanuenses, as Champsaur tended to hire them by the hour from an agency, which did not assist continuity of comprehension on the part of the secretaries. It is somewhat repetitive, and eccentrically punctuated, as well as occasionally omitting details of the plot that are subsequently employed as if they had been itemized. One even suspects that a slight malice might have crept into the relationship between the dictator and those taking his dictation on occasion, it being hard to think of another reason why the author would have required his employee repeatedly to spell out *amblyrhynchus* rather than simply calling the creature in question a marine iguana. More importantly, however, the book losses its continuity as it approaches its conclusion, and the final chapters are curt

and somewhat disordered, teetering on the edge of inco-
herency, although the author was clearly determined to
bring the work to the conclusion that he had planned.

In spite of those flaws, however, which were probably the effects of taxing illness, *L'Attirante* is certainly
worthy of attention, and not only because of the imaginative extravagance of the story, which displays an exu-
berant and sometimes blackly comic playfulness typical
of Champsaur's work. Like many of his later novels it
has more than a hint of pulp adventure fiction about it,
but it is also has his typical personal fascinations, in an
idiosyncratic amalgam.

Although it lacks the robust healthy musculature of
such eccentric *tours de force* as *Ouha, roi des singes*
(1923; tr. as *Ouha, King of the Apes*), *Homo-Deus: Le
Satyre Invisible* (1924; tr. as *Homo Deus*) and their joint
sequel *Nora la guenon devenue femme* (1929; tr. as *Nora
the Ape-Woman*), it is by no means a flaccid narrative,
and if its vigor is more than a little forced, it certainly
does not lack determination. The novel can be regarded
as a kind of afterthought to a bumpy career that had
passed its final peak, but precisely because of that it has
a particular interest as a kind of commentary on the artistic ambitions that the career in question had developed,
in an unrepentantly strange fashion.

This translation was made from a copy of the 1931
Ferenczi edition. The layout of that original text is eccentric, the last lines of many chapters often being dis-
placed to a subsequent page, after an arbitrary gap, in
order that each new chapter can always start on a odd-
numbered page without actually leaving any blank, but I
have not reproduced that quirk. I have also felt free to
amend the punctuation, on the assumption that much of

that supplied by the amanuensis might have been cor-
rected by the author had he been able to do so, but I suspect that his eyesight had deteriorated considerably and
that such corrections to the text as he did were based on
pages being read back to him rather than his actually
reading them. I hope and trust that he would thank me
for that assistance rather than cursing me for the slight
interference.

Brian Stableford

THE ALLURING

This book contains the story of a volcanic island in the Atlantic Ocean, which surged forth one day in eternity under the tropics, and disappeared on another day as it had been born.

It is like a grain of incense burned to an idol, WOMAN; that troubling fetish reigns on a little planet turning around a Sun, itself one of millions and millions of Suns illuminating infinite space, THE EARTH, where MAN lives, one intelligent force in the Kosmos, which is not.

Félicien Champsaur,
1931.

CHAPTER I
A Torpedoed Transatlantic Liner

Suddenly crushed by invisible submarine hands, an enormous transatlantic liner sank in the ocean. It carried with it its count of living beings; to wit, two hundred. They were, for the most part, young Frenchmen resident in Brazil, responding to the appeal of the endangered fatherland.

One day among many, therefore, the first of March 1915, saw another drama of the war: the majestic and superb Brazilian steamer *España*, and its passengers, became, at the whim of a German torpedo-boat, those rigid forms with which the waves play tennis. The balls that furrowed the water were human beings. The hull of the boat gave the impression of a net. Sirens with floating hair amused themselves singing and calling, sending the bodies back and forth.

Carried away, rolled among the cold cadavers and similar to them in appearance, one young man floated who was not entirely dead. The cork lifejacket had done its job; it retained at the surface the matter, deprived of consciousness, of the escapee: the only one.

He might have been twenty-six years old. His tall stature, his apparent muscles and his entire supple and vigorous being made him one of the finest human specimens. He had the slightly bronzed complexion of mixed race individuals, born to a Toulousan father and a Brazilian mother, with regular European features.

While the morning sun continued to rise over the ocean, Jean Harvez finally opened his eyes. He realized his terrible situation. Remembrance returned to him, seething with youth, and a flood of memories that, colliding in his weary head, made him physically ill.

Gradually, he succeeded in ordering his thoughts. He pictured the engulfment of the liner at dawn and the conditions of his shipwreck. He had gone up on deck, and had retired to an isolated spot under one of the lifeboats hanging from its davits, plunged in a profound meditation.

With a bleak obstinacy he was still dreaming about the same adventure, and doubtless the same amour: "*The Alluring...! Niña...! Niña...!*" like a thirsty man who, having already drunk too much, can no longer say anything but: "Water!" A lugubrious voice rose from the lounge, lulling his nostalgia without breaking his solitude.

Deprived of a bier
On the cold stone
Closing my eyes,
I seem to be asleep...

All of a sudden the ship received a mighty shock, which shook it. The angle of inclination of the floor augmented with an alarming rapidity. On the deck, a few passengers, having already emerged from their cabins, clung on to the rail or the equipment; they were howling: "Help!" The captain of the steamer and his officers tried to organize aid, but the vessel nose-dived so rapidly that it was impossible to put the lifeboat in the water.

Without trying to elucidate the causes of the accident, Jean understood immediately the inanity of means of assistance. He reached the officers' ward-room. There he saw numerous lifejackets. He took off his jacket, and then his shirt, and unhooked a lifejacket from the wall. Hastening to the rail, he leapt into the sea. He fell from a height of twenty meters. The water hissed in his ears violently.

He returned to the surface. The ship was sinking deliberately, it seemed to him.

The bold man shoved himself away from the hull with a furious kick and reached open water. Only the instinct of self-preservation was guiding him. What insensate hope did he have of escaping the catastrophe? It seemed to him that there did not exist, at that moment, any other law than that of death: no longer to think, no longer to feel.

Jean strove to remain alive, ran out of breath, and delivered himself to a passing wave.

The caressant hair of sirens balanced his departing body voluptuously.

The engines of the *España* were not yet drowned. The rear propeller was rotating with a frightful noise out of the water, and perhaps, by means of its whirling in the air, sustained the fine ship, which did not want to end, upright on its stem. The part out of the water was still brilliantly illuminated.

Suddenly, as if drawn, clutched by giant invisible fingers, the enormous steamer sank, carrying with it its entire complement of passengers, except one.

With rapid decision, Jean had recovered his senses fully. The sun was high above the horizon. When the wave lifted him up to its summit, he glimpsed the ocean in the space of a few seconds, the waves of which bristled one after another with a regular splashing. Then he went down again, and his view was limited to the extent of the water that bore him.

He tried to cry out, hoping that a voice might respond to his own, but the agitation of the waters was such that his words only carried a few meters, vain and utterly futile.

At each ascent he gazed around him avidly, but he only saw the ever-menacing immensity of the ocean, suddenly unleashed round the catastrophe of the magnificent vessel *España*, entirely drowned by a final trick of humans, swallowed body and contents in the watery abyss.

Suddenly, the sun disappeared, and a livid light covered the surface. At the same time, a devastating gust of wind fell.

As if lifted up by a colossal force, the waves leapt up, rising to a vertiginous height. In spite of his lifejacket, the handsome swimmer was picked up, rolled, and tumbled into the hollow of the wave like a toy kicked along by a capricious child.

I'm doomed! he thought. *I'd do better, instead of fighting for my life, to unfasten this lifejacket and let myself sink. The sea takes me for an enemy!*

But he was young, full of strength and audacity. There would always be time to abandon himself. After the malevolence of hostile humans, a torpedo-strike, there was the anger—no, the bad luck—of the elements: a tempest. To struggle is to live. The exhaustion of strength does not annihilate the will. Jean Harvez did not want to consent to the cowardice of his body, which was begging for mercy.

The more he lost his vigor, therefore, the more an appetite was born within him for risk and battle, tenacity against misfortune, the pride in victory that makes a man sublime and renders him heroic.

Stuck to his legs, the stiffened fabric of his trousers was embarrassing him horribly; he tried to take them off. After a terrible gust of wind, there was a calm. The shipwreck victim took advantage of it, bringing his feet up behind him, taking his boots off, one after the other; then, unbuckling the belt of his trousers, he rolled it up, with difficulty. Once the knees were passed, the task became easier, and the trousers went to join the footwear on the sea bed.

The hurricane was unleashed again, with an insensate fury. From then on the unfortunate was borne away, losing consciousness of the struggle, along with an exact notion of obstacles. He only had the instinct of gulping mouthfuls of air every time the wave lifted him up to its summit.

Fortunately, the young man had fastened the life-jacket securely under his arms, a precaution more than necessary; with the impacts inflicted on him by the furious sea, his head was more often under the water than above it.

Sometimes, lifted up to the crest of a gigantic wave, he was projected, and fell back into the water from a height of fifteen or twenty meters. Then, stunned and inanimate, he floated. Thought escaped him; he became inert matter, a simple item of wreckage delivered to the caprice of the squalls. In that rag rolled by the wind and suffocated by the foamy brine, however, the soul still lived.

In spite of corporeal suffering, the poor devil's agony was mingled with intimate dreams; tableaux and scenes arrived to add the anguish of memories to his momentary dolor.

He was in his studio, in Paris, a debutant sculptor already considered as a future master; he was modeling a bust. The model was smiling at him softly. He felt a juvenile tenderness inspire him, for the pure and smiling face was that of his mother.

Suddenly, a door opened and a young woman, brown-haired, white, beautiful and splendid, came in. A strange detail: she was naked, but did not seem to care. She approached, curious to see the artist's work; then, unceremoniously, she took the place of Madame Harvez, who disappeared. She posed.

The sculptor set to work furiously; the piece did not make progress. The clay slid under the soft shaper, almost fluid. The artist repeated his gesture without tiring. He looked at his model, but that model too faded away. Jean ran to the young woman in order to retain her, but she was diluted in his hands and he saw with horror that he was kneading an earthenware statue. A burst of laughter behind him made him turn round. She was there, superb, standing on the saddle, resuming the pose.

Furious, Jean ran to the woman, seized her and clasped her in his arms. He felt himself entering into her slowly; with a sentiment of superhuman sensuality, he melted into that magnificent body.

Jean no longer existed. In the studio, sovereignly, in a faultless marble statue, stood *The Alluring*.

In the midst of the spray, perched on the foamy swirl of the waves, The Alluring, perhaps his masterpiece, surged forth in her marvelous nudity: the body, so feminine, swathed in front, the arms falling toward the thighs in a gesture of appeal, the hands joined, their thumbs horizontal and the other fingers lowered and rigid, in the form of a yoni.[1] Simultaneously taking and refusing, in a last troubling defense, like a consenting and dominating offer, she seemed to be saying:

"I am Beauty, the immortal radium that is worth any sacrifice. Physical and mental sensuality resides in me. Mine is your intelligence, which has seen me, your art, which has created me, your will, which wanted me thus, and your soul, which animates me!

"My power surpasses that of living statues, stifled by clothing and conventions.

"In my attitude, in the pose of my legs crossed like Buddha, I am sitting on my rivals, the poor women who only know how to speak by making noise. I dominate by silence. My beauty speaks. My mysterious smile is an appeal to which everyone listens.

"In seeking to decipher my secret, one becomes my prisoner, and never my possessor.

"Repose your feverish head on my lap, man, my hands will part the divine triangle that they form in order to caress your weary brow.

"I am the idol that is adored, not the slave who serves her master on her knees.

"Now that you have realized that feminine, carnal and solar debauchery, The Alluring, you will no longer be able to submit to other laws than those of your creation.

---

[1] This pose, significant in terms of the novel's symbolism, is reproduced in the original edition in the cover illustration and in a line-drawing employed as a frontispiece, both by the artist Fabius Lorenzi, who provided illustrations for several of Champsaur's later works.

"Your model is nothing, you have expelled her. Your mother and your dead father cannot defend you against me. You love me as you have never loved.

"I am your creature and the sonorous and victorious, yet soft and tender, name of Nano, Nini—a variant in my country of 'little girl,' Niña—that you have given me, participates in your name, Jean, as my sculpted body comes to the gesture of your hands."

He saw himself in his studio again before his work, caressing it fearfully, kissing it devotedly, a new Pygmalion. A fury sometimes agitated him, throwing him breathlessly upon the sculpture in order to animate it, to clasp it, to warm up its coldness, to communicate his fever to it, in order that his creature might belong to her creator entirely.

Nano, The Alluring, was smiling at a vague dream, as inaccessible as if she were immaterial. Then Jean ran his tremulous fingers over the firm and beautiful curves of his creature, recognizing all the contours and charming corners kneaded with his amour, and he suffered with desire, to the point of going mad.

After having exhibited it at the Salon, he refused to sell his work to the State; and as his morbid passion began to be known and mocked, he abandoned Paris and his nascent glory in order to take shelter in Santos, where his mother had been born. He lived tranquilly there, hidden, working with more or less success on other works, which never equaled The Alluring. The war determined him to return to France. And the transatlantic liner *España*, in which he was sailing, had just been torpedoed while traversing the tropical waters.

Jean is still struggling against the tempests and his visions of fury. The ocean, whistling and blowing, is only danger revealed and danger to dread. After the visit of the ideal, The Alluring, the harassed shipwreck victim receives the more dangerous one of phantom ships. Is it a fever occasioned by the peril, the torpedo-strike, the wind, the turbulent ocean and the sun, terrible on a male and cerebral nudity? But that submarine warfare against a steamship evokes for him ancient petty struggles and great sea battles; they come, the accursed, in series, in all shapes and sizes, ironclads and sloops, triremes and galleys.

The impeccable crewmen and ragged fishermen make signals and gestures of appeal. The ocean is populated with fantastic rescuers. They are the souls of old ships lost during their wrecks that are passing by. At close range, Jean, who calls out, sees wooden skeletons maneuvered by human skeletons. It's all over; he is in the realm of nightmares and shades.

Here comes a three-master, and up above the figurehead, the prow and the masts, the arms of the mainmast, broken at the level of the impact, the halyards and the rigging. It launches forward to attack; then, crack, the bowsprit is ripped away. The ship is opened up. Jean is rolled by a wave and screams in horror.

It is a brig that follows, as neat as a jewel. Here comes a schooner, its captain making signs in the prow. Frigates pass by, steamers, ironclads, warships and merchant ships, centuries mingled.

Sounds of bells in the distance, knells.

Splashed by the surf, the wrecks are abandoned now in a bizarre procession; Jean's quasi-cadaver brushes them, soft and lugubrious, made of a wisp of fog; the spirits of the ocean push them toward an unknown goal, and the shadow devours them.

The water is mordant, crushing. Jean feels a thousand teeth, a thousand claws, strangulations and chokings harassing him. All his fibers have become cords of suffering. The naked man, still struggling in spite of everything, no longer has any but one impression, that of the tempest that is martyrizing him lamentably.

Hours have passed.

The equatorial sun, its radiance too ardent, burned a poor lost soul floating at the whim of the water, calm at present. Under the terrible bite, the sculptor recovered consciousness, but, devoid of strength and thought, he had the bewildered gaze of a moribund passing through his swollen eyelids.

Mechanically, he put his hands to his head for a few moments, but always, always, with the same mechanical movement, he brought his arms alternately one over the other.

The day went by like that. When the star descended over the horizon the ocean was completely calm and the waves were following one another, long and flat; the swell was mild and regular. With the night, a little peace descended over the shipwreck victim. How long had he been struggling against the tempest? He had no idea, but his exhaustion was extreme, and above all, the thirst that tormented him was becoming a torture. Even so, he held firm, very tiny and stark naked, in the immense ocean.

The night was bright and serene. In those tropical regions the air is so diaphanous that the stars give enough light to see a long way; the sea was deserted.

A comforting impression determined that Jean Harvez suddenly thought that he was heading toward a goal. It was more a sensation than a certainty. By virtue of an almost superhuman courage, he constrained himself then to judge coldly and envisage his situation.

He did not know of any land where he might be fortunate enough to come ashore.

The war, which had become torpedo warfare, in continuing that deadly game, would gradually reduce commercial navigation; thus, the chance of being picked up by a ship was slender. Increasingly, that minuscule nothing, a man at sea, could only be spotted by a miracle.

Wait, then? Continue suffering?

Tomorrow, could he bear the implacable tortures of the sun for another day? No, undoubtedly. Better to finish it, then.

He consented to his defeat. Vitality gradually withdrew from him. Jean Harvez gave up.

The probable death was slow in coming. He was about to hasten to meet it. He put his last resources of strength into unfastening his lifejacket. The swollen leather did not lend itself to that easily; twisted and rolled around the cork rectangle, it doubled the difficulty. Jean had to lacerate it piece by piece. A singular condition of the shipwreck-victim; it was now necessary to toil in order to have the right to die.

There were only three thongs to untie; it took two hours. Finally, the last one gave way. In the dark, thought almost escaped him; no longer anything but an object, a wisp delivered to all the unconscious forces of nature, he was a human rag, burned by the day's sun, rolled by the interminable ocean. In a supreme surge, he held on to the lifejacket for a moment; then, pushing it away, he let himself sink...

CHAPTER II
A Man Saved, Perhaps

When Jean allowed himself to sink, an intense se-renity penetrated him, a radiation; to the wellbeing of his flesh, liberated from the lifejacket, which had become a dolorous matrix, was added the ferocious satisfaction of his heroism, which had not consented to let go.

Then he started swimming underwater, in order to play with death and test his strength.

Completely naked, he felt lightened of all hypocri-sies. It is at such moments, often, that a man is revealed to himself. He was thinking for the last time.

Jean had had the honors, almost the glory, of an art-ist, the amour offered on the plate of wealth. He had al-lowed himself to live elegantly, but he had understood that he was capable of better than such frills. He felt that he was a prisoner of that former attitude, as if enclosed in a luxurious box; it was at that moment that Jean re-gretted, not the life that was fleeing him, but the one that he had been able to live, overburdened with needs and contests.

He had a desire to be a human animal confronting primitive nature, a fighter, with no armor but his breast, no defense but his hands. The war to which he was going might have made him the man that he wanted to be, whereas now...

Now, he encounters a point of support. He clings to it, twists, extends the other foot. He feels solidity beneath him. He stands up; he walks. His upper body emerges from the water. He can finally breathe. He sees a dark mass silhouetted by the lunar light.

He hears the familiar sound of waves breaking on reefs.

The rugged, uneven ground tears the soles of his feet. It's a bank of coral. He advances slowly, lest he disappear into abysses between the polyps.

Jean senses his strength quitting him. He wants to arrive while he can still defend himself; he runs recklessly, fall, gets up again and sets forth again.

He finally reaches the nearby shore, a sandy beach on to which he throws himself voluptuously and rolls, a poor unconscious mass, but saved from the immense mass of salt water rumbling around him in the starry darkness.

The whole night passes by thus, in reparative sleep.

The sun had already warmed the sand where the man lay.

An enormous crab, emboldened by the immobility of the castaway, quits its damp abode, and with its oblique march, approaches the inanimate body. The left leg tempts it; it seizes a shred near the toe.

Jean shuddered violently and woke up.

That dolor extracted him from a torpor that, in that latitude, would inevitably have terminated in death.

The crab, frightened, had fled. Once the first moment of dizziness had passed, Jean came to, and dragged himself into the shelter of an enormous rock that projected an expanse of shadow over the ground. Once protected from the terrible sun, he was able to examine the place where he was.

The strip of sand on which he had fallen might have been a hundred meters wide. It was bounded by high cliffs that extended to the left all the way to the sea. Cracked and fissured, advancing over the sand in enormous granite buttresses, they seemed quite inaccessible. To the right, the cliff continued, forming a vast circle, part of which—the part where our hero had come ashore—had collapsed. The nature of the cliffs was entirely composed of volcanic rocks, granite and mica, large streaks of which sparkled in the sunlight, a complicated glitter of diamonds with warm tones, as nacreous as pearls.

The vast magical circle was the crater of a volcano, certainly the shaper of the island. The portion turned toward the sea, undermined by the waves for centuries, had ended up sinking beneath the water. The waves had invaded the former crater and formed a lake, the inky black water of which indicated the immense depth.

Toward the right, after the lake in the crater, the cliff continued. Its height, which Jean estimated approximately, might have been four hundred meters at the highest point. It extended almost equally nearly all the way to the horizon. That cliff was confounded in a chaos of enormous rocks, colossal landsides extending all the way to the sea. Beyond, Jean could perceive the commencement of a sandy beach bristling with enormous blocks of stone. It was easy to see that the massive landslip extended over a rather large area, because its point, forming reefs, was frayed by the ocean.

At the place where Jean had come ashore, the sea, at low tide, permitted the sight of the surface of a bank of coral, the branches of which continued their entanglements as far as the eye could see, like an immense forest with motionless branches.

Jean had recovered all his faculties. The voyages he had already made and his knowledge of natural laws, equipped him better than most people to struggle against any adversity. He had a physical need to live; it had served him.

Alone, without weapons, without any garment, he was hungry and thirsty, his body bruised, his feet bloody. He envisaged his lamentable situation clearly, without trembling, and felt ready to fight.

He might have said, like Ajax, "I shall be victorious, in spite of the gods." But Jean, the son of a free-thinker, hostile to any religious idea, had been brought up outside vain beliefs. He admired the work of nature, but did not seek to put a name to the marvelous unsigned work. Understanding that the human mind is not yet mature enough to define the mystery of terrestrial life, he deemed that his duty was always to elevate himself by the toil of the body and the brain, thus preparing the way for the future race destined to understand the supreme goal and reign over the earth.

That slow power of divination, developed from one century to the next, would gradually bring creatures to rejoin the creative Spirit and only to be one with it.

His pride did not rise as far as supposing himself worthy to enter into communication via prayer with the Supreme Being, but he sensed that in struggling against poverty and death he was fulfilling the duty of human-kind—destined, as natural laws seemed to indicate, to be the master of the globe.

In order to appease the thirst that seemed to him to be the most urgent of his needs, he thought that the torrential rain of the recent tempest must have left a little water in a few hollows in the rocks. He climbed painfully to the foot of the cliff, fortunately in shadow, and set

about exploring the base. The search was long and difficult, but he finally heard a slight splashing that filled
him with hope and courage.

Into a veritable natural cistern, the water was trick-
ling, forming a thin silvery thread over the granite surface, sliding there, following all its sinuosities, to end in
a kind of shallow bowl scarcely deeper than a meter and
three meters wide. Jean drank until he was sated, and
then bathed himself, immediately finding a great relief.
His skin, impregnated with salt water, was burning him,
torturing him with inflamed points. Then he sprinkled
fine sand on the wound in his foot; the blood had flowed
to the extent of leaving a ruddy brown streak. Then he
returned to the sea and searched for a few shellfish in
order to calm his hunger.

It did not take him long to find some. The reefs,
now out of the water, were covered by a species with
oval shells, incurved on one side, striated with broad
grooves and ridges, decorative in appearance. They were
lamellibranch mollusks, known as a trigonioids, with a
geniculate foot that served for crawling and jumping, the
taste of which is similar to our mussels, but which are
much larger.[2]

Without going into the water Jean was able to collect a hundred, which he placed in the sun. He withdrew
to the shadow of a rock and waited. The wait was not
long, only a few minutes. In the ardent heat the
trigonioids opened. Jean ran, took one, found it exquisite, and continued; in a few minutes his meal was fin-

---

[2] It is surprising, given that the narrative voice can identify the
mollusks with this degree of specificity, that he does not men-
tion that trigonioids had supposedly been extinct for millions
of years, the identified species being Mesozoic fossils.

ished. He could have eaten twice as many, but it was impossible for him to remain exposed to the sun's rays any longer. He returned to his cistern, drank avidly, and then, spotting a block that formed a screen, he slid into its shelter and immediately fell asleep.

When he awoke it was dark. He felt somewhat rested, and, emerging from his shelter, he started walking, still very painfully, his bare bruised feet causing him considerable suffering.

It was one of those beautiful tropical nights when the air is so transparent that innumerable constellations illuminate as much as a magnificent moonlight.

Jean sat down on a rock at the edge of the sea and reflected on what he could do. It was futile to try to scale the cliff in the place where he was; he was still too weak and his bruised limbs would have refused him their offices. However, it was absolutely necessary for him to reach a high point in order to judge the place where he was.

Was he on an island? An island seemed the most plausible hypothesis. It remained to reach the far side of the drowned crater and reach the summit of the cliffs by scaling a landslide, if he did not have the strength to reach the sandy beach he had seen the day before. But he was hungry again. He returned to his larder—which is to say, to the rocks that bore the trigonioids. Those rocks, exposed the day before, were now under water. He went into the water shoulder-deep and reached the shellfish quite easily; he collected a large quantity, which he threw on to the beach as he went along, for he had not the slightest piece of cloth from which he could make an envelope.

When he judged that he had taken enough he returned to the shore and, having reassembled them, prepared to eat them. A difficulty of which he had not thought presented itself. The day before the heat of the sun had made them open, but it was now impossible for him to achieve that. He tried to hammer them against the rocks without result. He had to crush them between two stones, but then he broke them and the mollusk, flattened and mingled with the debris of its shell, was inedible. Nevertheless, he had to content himself temporarily with that slow means. He contrived thus to ward off his hunger rather than satisfying it.

Time was passing, and Jean was not unaware that he ought to profit from the hours of the night to do something. The night, the early hours of the day and the last few were the only times when the heat was tolerable, so he made the decision to act without further delay. He returned to the cistern, which he found half empty; the water that remained was warm and polluted. He drank anyway, and bathed again, which did him good; his wounds had scabbed and were making him suffer.

When he had finished, he saw with terror that the trickle of water had dried up. It was, therefore, even more necessary for him to quit that inhospitable beach and reach the other side of the cliffs. He returned to the edge of the seas; there he identified the shortest route to reach the landslides. He saw the Black Lake; he gave it that name because the water seemed inky, making a contrast with the gold of the stars, which was reflected there as if in an immense mirror.

The diameter of the former crater appeared to be about three hundred meters. At any other time Jean would have made a game out of swimming it, but in his present state of exhaustion he had to think of taking advantage of the configuration of the old volcano. Instead of traversing it directly in its greatest diameter, he judged it more prudent to do so by gaining the various spurs of rock successively. They emerged from the sea, the remains of the ancient chimney of the volcano.

He was about to throw himself into the water when a slight sound behind him caused him to turn round. It came from the heap of shellfish that had served as his frugal meal. He saw, distinctly, something gray agitating amid the debris. He armed himself with a large stone and approached, crawling slowly; but he was heard, for he suddenly saw a large crab taking flight.

Jean threw his stone at it, and was fortunate enough to hit it. The animal was stunned momentarily; that sufficed for him to catch up with it and break its enormous claws, which reduced it to impotence. It was a decapod with a carapace as long as it was broad, terminating with several articulated feet and provided, like lobsters, with a formidable pair of formidable pincers. Although the crustacean weighed at least three kilos, Jean had butchered it in no time at all and ate it.

That nourishment, passably indigestible, nevertheless reinforced the young man. He reserved the two claws, which constituted half the total weight in themselves. With one in each hand he set forth to brave the water, swimming toward a islet situated a hundred meters away. A few minutes later, he reached it, rested for a while and departed for another islet situated about the same distance away. He repeated that operation again and lay down wearily on a shore in order to rest before finishing his crossing. From the point where he was he could see the whole of the lake, and a sort of vertigo afflicted him as he gazed at the reflected stars. One might have thought that he was placed between two skies, offering the same immense profundity above and below to his vision.

At that moment, without anything appearing to trouble the surface of the water, it seemed to him that he saw a white shadow gliding at a great depth. He raised his head, thinking that a cloud was passing above him, but the sky was pure. He lowered his eyes to the lake again; the shadow continued to glide near the bottom, heading for a point opposite the one where he was located, confined by the cliffs.

A little beneath the surface of the water, he perceived through the transparency, a large black hole; the white shadow went toward that hole, plunged into it and disappeared.

He thought that it must be the entrance to a submarine cavern. A slight frisson ran over his epidermis, and he hesitated momentarily before getting into the water again. He could not stay where he was, however. Jean let himself slide, as silently as possible, and resumed swimming prudently.

He had crossed two thirds of the distance when having arrived level with the mysterious shadow, terror seized him. He hastened his movements, and his fear increased along with his velocity. A terrible anguish, such as he had never felt before, gripped his heart and stifled him, tensed his limbs and labored his sides.

Finally, he reached a beach of small stones and polyp debris. He launched himself forward, without worrying about anything that might hurt his feet, and ran for about twenty meters.

At that moment a dry click, like the crack of a whip, resounded behind him, followed by a foamy splash. He turned round but he only saw long ripples on the surface of the water. A malaise held him motionless, pensively for a long moment.

Then he shrugged his shoulders, and departed in search of discoveries.

CHAPTER III
Discoveries Made While Going Along

The place that Jean had just reached was rocky, furrowed by crevices extending into the distance. They fell steeply one above another and formed gigantic steps rising all the way to the summit of the ancient volcano. An embryonic natural stairway, the steps of which were ten or fifteen meters high, went all the way to the sea.

To the left, the disposition was the same as at the beginning of the formation of the island, but a further eruption had caused a dislocation of the hillside. There was nothing but a heap of monstrous rocks piled up pell-mell, all the way to the summit of the crater; it was that summit that it was necessary to attain in order to assess the place where he was and get his bearings for a permanent installation.

He therefore set out to follow the base of the volcano; fearful of getting lost among the enormous blocks, he followed the sea shore. He was obliged to retrace his steps several times because the route he took led into a cul-de-sac. Nevertheless, from one meander to another he ascended, and after four hours he reached the summit of the volcano.

A sad spectacle was then offered to his sight. Disengaged from the mass of rocks that cluttered the base of the seashore, it rose up conically for about four hundred meters. The igneous matter had escaped through a long regular corridor. On the landward side, the volcano offered an absolute contrast with that turned toward the infinite sea, as unified here as it as ragged there. From the summit of the crater, a series of increasingly low undulations departed to the left, finishing in hillocks all the way to the extreme horizon. All of it was arid, bleak and desolate, granite extending in broad sweeps, like petrified waves. To the right, it was terminated by the fracture that had given birth to the cliffs bordering the ocean.

If that chain of hills were the dorsal spine of a volcanic island, as everything seemed to indicate, very few resources remained. He wanted to make sure of that, and, going around the volcanic cone, he headed for the sequence of hills. An hour later, he reached the peak. From there, his view embraced a vast area. In the distance, parallel to the one he had just attained, another similar chain extended. Between the two he saw a deep valley which appeared to be two or three kilometers wide. It was evident that the hills had been born during the upheaval of the ground caused by interior fires, first extending around the volcanic cone, supported thereon, and drawing further apart like the spokes of an immense wheel of which the crater was the hub.

At that moment a soft light came to silhouette the gigantic forms, and shortly afterwards, the moon rose over the desolate landscape.

In the direction of the volcano, then perfectly illuminated, Jean could only distinguish torn-up rocks, furrowed by deep fissures; their bizarre profiles were cut out fantastically against the luminous background. Two of those rocks, thin and vertical, had the silhouette of two women in the process of gossiping. Another looked like an ape. On the opposite side, a light mist veiled the landscape.

The moon, continuing its ascension, came to illuminate the depths of the valley. Jean uttered a cry of joy.

There, in the deepest part, a sinuous line extended. Might that be the fresh water so much desired, so much sought?

Water: which is to say, life—and possibly vegetation.

He descended from the heights, heading toward that goal, which contained, for him, the most precious and refreshing cordial he could find. It took him about two hours to attain it, his bruised feet caused him to suffer so much. On the way he encountered several thorny plants, cacti of a sort.

Finally, he reached the river. Yes, it really was a river, seven or eight meters wide, profoundly framed by granite banks. He did not have the patience to search for a place that was less steep; letting himself slide down the rocky slope, he rolled into the beneficent water, in which he bathed voluptuously. The current was almost insensible. Strangely enough, instead of flowing toward the sea it went toward the volcano.

When he stood up, the man found that he only had water up to his shoulders. The bed was composed of fine sand, only a few centimeters thick.

Refreshed by the bath and his thirst calmed, he decided to go upstream, hoping that that region might be richer in vegetation. In any case, swimming in that warm water was a veritable pleasure, especially by comparison with the suffering he endured while walking. He therefore followed the river to his right. He moved rapidly, while observing the banks in order to find a landing point. The bed was the bottom of a narrow fissure and its limits offered the same steepness everywhere. From time to time he encountered other fractures, from which thin streams of water came to aliment the river.

Jean was an excellent swimmer, so he judged, after a certain time, that he had covered four or five kilometers.

He emerged into a lake—or, rather, a kind of near-circular hole. It was like a well, doubtless a petty chimney of the volcano that the water had been able to fill before finding an outflow through the crack. There the current no longer existed. Jean estimated the diameter of the lake as thirty meters; its somber tint indicated a great depth.

After having examined the strange place, he judged it appropriate to retrace his route as far as one of the tributaries and to follow it in order to find a means of reaching the bank.

Suddenly, his head bumped into a floating object. Jean looked, and saw a small black mass nearby. He grabbed it, and his heard bounded with hope in his breast. It was a coconut!

Coconut palms! He was saved!

CHAPTER IV
The Four Coconut Palms

In order to comprehend the joy experienced by Jean at the sight of the coconut it is necessary to know all the different resources of the palm tree that produced it. Those of the majority of its relatives were limited to a fruit and a little foliage, a shade always sought in hot countries, but the coconut palm itself, in addition to its large leaves, contains numerous resources, to such an extent that on certain islands, along with fish, it supplies all the needs of the aborigines.

Its fruit, the nut, is a complete aliment, healthy and substantial; the liquid it contains, known as coconut milk, has an agreeable taste. One can obtain a greasy substance from it, coconut butter, which serves as a preparation for all aliments. At the center of its branches a bud grows, the palm cabbage, which cedes nothing in quality to European cabbages, the taste of which is even finer. Its wood, very consistent, serves for the construction of a cabin, and its leaves to cover it. The fibers of the ribs of those leaves make very pretty and very solid baskets.[3] The purse of sorts that contains the nut, when

---

[3] The term I have translated here as "rib" is *nervure*, which is sometimes also translated as "vein." That of the palm-leaf is, indeed, very fibrous; that creates a problem because it is difficult to find a better English word than "fiber" to describe the hairy projections on the outside of the coconut, which Champsaur describes as *bourre* [stuffing]. Henceforth I have used "rib" for any fibrous rod or string extracted from the

worked, supplies fiber for somewhat coarse but solid cloth. Finally, making use of the two concave halves of the nut, one has receptacles capable of containing food and drink.

One can therefore judge the contentment of the young adventurer when he encountered the fruit of the precious plant. Pushing the marvelous nut in front of him, he set out in quest of a landing in order to go in search of the coconut palm. He had to swim for a long time, however, before finding an accessible place. It had been easy to throw himself into the river, but getting out of it easily was a very different matter.

The bed was, in sum, merely a crevice, the bottom of which was partly filled in by stones and sand. Over time, the terrible tropical hurricanes than swept the isle at certain times had dragged those stones and that and into all the cracks. Gradually, the bed of the watercourse had evened out, but its sides were as abrupt as they had been at the formation of the fissure. It was only at the intersection of two rips in the ground that the castaway was finally able to hoist himself out of the river, holding the famous nut preciously under his arm.

For the second time he quit the liquid domain for secure footing; but it was, alas, a bitter disappointment. As far as his eyes could see, there was nothing but masses of sterile blocks of stone or long sandy plains. However, that nut could not have fallen into the river without there being a tree that had previously produced it.

It's necessary, Jean thought, *that I scale the mountain, in order to have a view of the whole and know whether I truly am on an island.*

---

leaves and reserved "fiber" for the padding made from the latter, in order to avoid ambiguity.

For the moment, the most urgent thing was to refresh himself. He still had the two crab pincers, thus far carried over his shoulders, one clutching the other, for he was not even the possessor of a piece of string. He had his famous coconut, but no implement with which to open it. Then he recalled the means employed by crabs that are very fond of those fruits; they find a means of feeding on it by introducing one of their claws into the peduncle and turning it in such a fashion as gradually to wear away and enlarge the opening. Jean had the pincers in question, but he judged that a sharp stone would be more suitable, of which there was no lack in that location.

He found what he needed, and succeeded in opening the dear nut without too much difficulty.

It was full of a whitish liquid, which he drank with an animal joy. Then he ate his two crab pincers, and concluded his meal with half of his nut. The taste and freshness of the fruit demonstrated to him that it had not been floating in the river for long; otherwise, the milk would have been thick and the flesh of the nut rancid.

As he finished his meal a faint light in the east indicated that daylight was imminent and that he needed to find a shelter. It was too late to return to his point of departure. Where he was, finding a refuge would be rather problematic. He therefore decided to return to the river and to spend the hottest part of the day plunged in the water. The steep banks assured him of an expanse of shadow.

He stood up and looked around. While searching for his stone he had drawn away from his landing point. To his left he saw a slight depression. He ran to it, but when he arrived on the edge he saw that he had been mistaken, and that a great plain of sand extended before him.

He was about to trace his steps when a bizarre accumulation in the distance attracted his attention. He went that way, and applauded himself for having done so. Some fifteen coconut palms lay scattered on the sand. He understood the cause: the last hurricane, or perhaps a whirlwind, had uprooted the group and now they were lying there, intermingled.

A few, partly sheltered by the last to fall, did not appear to have dried out yet and were adhering to the soil by their roots. Jean resolved to try and rescue them. He began by shifting the desiccated specimens, taking great care to arrange the palms on the ground. Then he collected the nuts, of which he found forty-seven, a veritable treasure trove. After that, he disengaged the trunks, making use of the lightest as a lever in order to move the others. The sun was already high in the sky. Fortunately, Jean had made a copious meal; otherwise, fatigue and need would have rendered the labor unsupportable. So, as soon as he had succeeded in straightening up four coconut palms, and had maintained them sufficiently, he covered his nuts and palms with sand in order that they would not be dispersed by a gust of wind. Having set aside a wad of coconut fiber, which he took with him, he hastened to return to the river and seek a refuge from the sun in its waters.

He was fortunate enough to discover, almost at water level, a crack in which he could nestle. Lying down in his cage of stone, in the cool shade, he drank, after having laid out the coconut fiber, which served him as a mattress, and he went to sleep blissfully for the first time since his shipwreck.

He woke up shortly before nightfall, and while waiting for the darkness to become complete he wove an eccentric rope about five meters long with some of the fiber. Its torsion was rather summary, but such that it might suffice and last for a few days.

He would have liked to make a pair of espadrilles with that rope, but having no thread or a needle with which to sew them he was obliged to limit himself to fabricating soles of a sort. He attached one to the underside of each of his feet with a cord that he made as thin as possible. It was very imperfect, but he found himself more comfortable and could walk with more assurance

Night had fallen; he went back to the cove of the coconut palms, thus designated because the sandy plain where he had found them was at the intersection of the river and one of its tributaries.

Jean resolved firmly that night to follow the river to its mouth. After having attached his shoes to his head to avoid getting them wet, he swam, examining the surroundings carefully.

After two hours he reached the base of the mountain. He thought that the river would wind around it in order to flow into the sea on the other side. Nothing of the sort: the current accelerated slightly, and then the man saw the watercourse divide between two enormous cubes of stone. He heard the sound of a waterfall. Not wanting to have the same fate as the river, he gained the bank at that point, formed by landslides, and, fraying a path through enormous rocks, he reached the entrance of a narrow fissure that rose all the way to the summit of the volcanic cone. That crevice was the same one as the river bed—or, rather, its point of departure.

What formidable eruption must have occasioned such a rip? At any rate, the effect and the cause were only too visible, and Jean understood that all the water falling in the region was concentrated in this natural reservoir, the lowest point. He could now hear the sound of the river inside the crater very distinctly. He tried to follow its course, but inside the fissure there was thick darkness.

He therefore retraced his steps and examined the opening of the bizarre defile. On the side where he was, he noticed a hollow at a height of about six meters that, seen from below, resembled a cave. He resolved to reach it and sought a means. An enormous cube was nearby; he went around it and saw that it was accessible toward the interior. He reached the base and, clambering from rock to rock, climbed it easily, the river becoming a thin stream.

Having arrived at the summit he did, in fact, see a cave, the entrance of which was at his level and no more than sixty centimeters away. Jean crossed that distance and penetrated into the grotto, illuminated then by moonlight.

The cave was very deep; twenty meters from the opening it was lost in obscurity. The floor was covered with a very fine and very dry sand. Jean was astonished to find such a thick layer of sand above the river and the surrounding plain, but he resolved to take advantage of it, without asking too many questions for the moment, and make it his general headquarters. By day he would be sheltered there from the sun and the heat, and would thus be able to work without risking sunstroke.

As he still had eight hours of night before him, he decided to begin transporting his booty to his new domicile. He went back down, and, after having taken his bearings well, he returned to the water and swam to the cove of the coconut palms. He reflected on the way, on what he was about to do, so that when he arrived he would only have to act.

Jean had to extend a layer of palms, arrange the rest of his fiber thereon with a few coconuts, fold over the palms so as to make a bale tied up by his long rope, load the whole on to his back, and, this time, follow the route on foot.

He examined his four coconut palms; they had resumed contact with the soil and seemed to be reconquering their vigor there.

At that moment, he heard a slight sound behind him and, on turning round, was stupefied.

CHAPTER V
The Struggle for Existence

Emerging from beneath the pile of palms, a sort of large lizard, or, rather, an iguana, raised itself up on its hind legs, gazing at him stupidly. Jean was very erudite in physical science and natural history, and he immediately recognized an amblyrhynchus,[4] an iguanid saurian reptile of the Americas, which sometimes attains a meter in length and weighs between fifteen and twenty kilos. Its skin is a dirty black, its head, broad and hooked, resembles that of a turtle. Its gait on land is rather slow; on the other hand, it is surprisingly agile in water, swimming by means of its tail, flattened at the sides.

Jean did not hesitate for a second. He leapt upon the reptile and clutched it between his knees; then, seizing its head, he tipped it backwards abruptly, thus breaking its vertebral column.

Then the orders of the day regarding labor changed. It was necessary to get back as soon as possible to Bon Repos—the name he gave, with all the force of his fatigue, to the cave—and proceed with the butchery of the reptile. The latter was one of the largest of its species, and weighed at least twenty kilos. Jean wrapped it up in

---

[4] *Amblyrhynchus* is the genus to which the "marine iguana" of the Galapagos islands is assigned. The Galapagos islands are in the Pacific rather than the Atlantic, so the presence of such a creature on Harvez Island is anomalous, but that is far from being the only anomaly of natural history in the story—which Jean's vaunted erudition never allows him to notice.

four beautiful palms, linked two nuts by their peduncles, which he passed over his shoulder one in front and one behind, put his parcel on top and set forth courageously.

He was strongly tempted, instead of following the river, to take a shorter route, but he feared encountering difficulties and put off that attempt until another day, when he could depart rested and without a burden.

He returned to Bon Repos well before sunrise. He went back down in order to search for a few trenchant stones, and succeeded in finding several. One of them seemed appropriate to make an ax. He took advantage of the last moments of the night to take some water up to his dwelling in an empty coconut. It could hold about a liter. Then he set to work, tranquilly. He contrived quite easily to butcher the amblyrhynchus and slice it up as thinly as possible. He took the slices to lay them out on a rock exposed to the sun. Having done that, he breakfasted on a coconut, and then lay down and went to sleep.

He woke up toward dusk, and remained lying down for a moment, reflecting.

He was vaguely conscious of having heard an unusual sound as he awoke. He listened for a few minutes, and the sound was repeated. It was coming from far away—very far away—in the depths of the cave, in the dark place that he had not yet explored. By day the cave was more brightly illuminated. Jean got up and headed toward the depths of his abode.

The volcano was decidedly not a poser of enigmas; its construction and deformation were explicable with childish simplicity. The cave was only one of numerous chimneys of the volcano, and the enormous rock that had served to climb up to it was fitted to it like a stopper. An expansion of gas must have done that work, chasing before it the rocks that opposed its emergence.

At the back, a sort of gallery opened, very steeply, which appeared to plunge into the entrails of the earth. The ground, strewn with small shards or rock, was not mixed with sand there. Jean crawled along, feeling the ground in front of him. After ten meters or so, the darkness becoming increasingly opaque, he judged it prudent to turn back.

At that moment, the sound he had heard was repeated. It was still very distant, but perfectly distinct. It reminded him of his emergence from the black lake; it resembled a violent whiplash striking water.

Having returned, he examined the cave attentively, and ended up discovering the provenance of the sand that carpeted Bon Repos. Three meters above, on the side opposite the chimney, a gaping opening appeared in the wall seven or eight meters from the opening to the exterior. When formidable storms raged, as they do in five months out of twelve in the tropical zone, diluvian rain eroded the rocky surface of the island incessantly. During the elevation of the land, the siliceous part that formed the sea bed had been brought to the surface, washed it in solution, and had been deposited in all the fissures capable of retaining it. Pouring down the slopes of the volcano, the water had drawn away everything that did not have the weight to resist it. The rolling stones wore one another away and were converted into sand and shingle.

Think about the immense quantities of sand that cover a part of the continents on the edge of the sea and the bottom of rivers and streams. What is that sand? The product of a disintegration, an end and not a beginning, coming from rocks, and then from their debris, pebbles that, having rolled incessantly, are worn away, becoming sands whose color depends on the nature of the rocks that gave birth to them. Thus, on the earth, nothing is immobile or immutable. That sand will become rock again, submissive to the influence of interior heat; condensed, it might be granite or porphyry again. Nothing dies, everything is transformed. Thus Jean thought, in gazing at the structure of his habitation, which became brighter and brighter.

Evidently, the grotto was only the point of emergence of a volcanic chimney. The central cone was doubtless the primordial chimney, but other explosions, other pulses of lava or vapor had given birth to other chimneys; the one in which he found himself must have been caused by a gaseous fury that, dislocating the stone and expelling the blocks, had formed the shelter where he was. The block that had permitted him to enter it was one of the rocks that had once occupied the interior. Other galleries, doubtless, must radiate through the mountain, higher up, and communicate with the exterior, since that was the route by which the sand carpeting the cave had arrived.

Jean put off until later a disciplined exploration. The most urgent thing was to bring all his provisions together and render them safe. For the moment, that was sufficient to permit him to plan certain tasks.

Night was approaching. He went out to collect his slices of iguana, by now perfectly dried. After a copious meal, composed of a single dish, the reptile, he headed for the coconut palms.

This time, his feet being in a better state, he decided to attempt the adventure across the plain. As usual, the night was perfectly bright and he could see a long way. At first he was surprised not to hear the slightest splash of water when he arrived at the river bank, but he understood the reason for it: the level had dropped to such an extent that it was no longer flowing through the crevice. Thus, there was no longer any doubt; the river was, in sum, merely the overflow of a reservoir. If the dry spell lasted long enough, the river would dry up completely. Fortunately, there was the reservoir in the middle, of such depth that water must never be lacking there. Would it be necessary for him to travel three or four kilometers in order to obtain water?

He found his way easily enough in that direction. The plain was almost entirely sandy, apart from a few enormous blocks looming up here and there like markers providing reference points to facilitate his return.

After two hours of walking he perceived his coconut palms on the horizon, animating the desert with a semblance or verdure. Half an hour later, he reached them, and saw with satisfaction that they appeared to be in good health.

He went then to see his buried provisions and freed them from the sand. He laid out a few palms, flattened over a layer of fiber, and then six nuts, folded over the palms and tied up the whole with his rope. Then Jean made a bale weighing about ten kilos. He dared not overload himself in view of the length of the road to travel. Nevertheless, before departure, he made his inventory again. In addition to the six nuts he was transporting, he still had forty-five nuts, a hundred and twenty-eight palms and some fifty kilos of fiber.

He gathered everything at the base of the four coconut palms, in such a fashion that nothing could deteriorate, with the nuts underneath in order that they would dry out as little as possible. For the moment, the four surviving coconut palms were devoid of fruit.

He loaded his bale on to his shoulder and set out again for Bon Repos. He reached it without difficulty well before sunrise.

After a meal composed of dried meat and a slice of coconut, washed down with coconut milk, he decided to employ part of the day in fitting out the cave. He began by clearing the floor. He made his bed in a sort of niche, extending a good layer of fiber over the fine sand. He had chosen the highest part of the cave, for the influx of sand seemed to indicate that on stormy days it was possible that the cavern might be partially flooded. Then he arranged his nuts and his meat in a crevice that was almost horizontal, placed about a meter and a half above the floor.

All that took about two hours. At that moment the heat outside had become intolerable, but inside the fissure it was quite bearable. Jean congratulated himself for having selected it as his domicile.

The most urgent matter was footwear; his soles, too summary, were already in tatters. For want of a needle it was necessary to find a substitute. He therefore set about spinning his fiber into the finest possible thread. He planted the strongest rib of a palm in the sand and attached the fragment of thread to it. He worked thus until about ten o'clock. He had made marks on the rock in accordance with the progress of the shadow, in such a way as to measure the division of time. Being in the tropical zone, sunrise varied very little from day to day.

In three hours he had had about eight meters of thread about as thick as a matchstick; it would therefore take him many hours to have a quantity sufficient to make a pair of soles. That tedious labor did not please him, and he decided only to devote a few hours to it every day. In the meantime, he enveloped his feet in the skin of the reptile, the amblyrhynchus—not very solid, to be sure, but which might last for a few days of walking. Afterwards, rest until five o'clock; resume interior work until moonrise, which happened about eight o'clock in the evening; an excursion in the island until sunrise; return to the dwelling; interior labor, etc.

Occupied with his physical needs, Jean was no longer thinking about his troubled mind. This primitive life of incessant struggle realized his mental salvation: a true miracle, made by a strange collaboration of all human and natural forces against the spiritual. How long would Jean's soul remain subordinate to the island? His former submission, to Nano, The Alluring, Nini, diminished, proving its impotence. Now he felt tall before this nature, tamed by him.

He was no longer the blasé sculptor, spoiled by the joys offered from all directions. He was a young animal, happy to bend his supple limbs to the most ordinary manual tasks.

Under the pressure of his desire, the dead, passive island became active, with its possibilities of shelter, nourishment and clothing. The first moment of alarm having passed, Jean felt that he was the master of a world, almost equal to a god.

And yet, how many dangers lay in wait for that insecurely seated divinity?

CHAPTER VI
The Turtle Eggs

Seven days went by in that fashion, which, with the six previous ones, added up to thirteen, the number of days already spent on the island: seven days, the monotony of which went by, full of continual labor. The provision of thread increased slowly; implementation was also in progress. Jean had made a kind of club with a stone fixed to the end of two palm ribs bound together, and then an ax, with a flat stone patiently sharpened by friction against the rugged granite and then fitted with a handle like the club. Another long, flat stone had been similarly sharpened in the form of a cutter, and another as a punch. He could now cleave his coconuts into two neat parts, which gave him receptacles.

Thus, in the thirteenth day of isolation, Jean departed to look for the rest of his harvest of coconuts. This time, he had made a sight detour, following the edge of the sea, when his attention was attracted by tracks visible in the fine sand forming the shore.

Jean was not in doubt for a minute. A large turtle had passed that way very recently; the imprints seemed to be fresh. Jean was armed with his ax. He therefore set out in search of the animal, resolved to master it. As far as his view extended, he could not see anything. On the ground, however, by studying it attentively, the traces clearly indicated the coming and going of the animal. To follow the return was futile; the turtle could not be attacked in the sea.

It was the egg-laying season; the interesting matter was to discover where the eggs were deposited. That was not very difficult; all the tracks ended in a little mound of sand. Carefully, Jean laid bare about a hundred eggs, freshly laid—an interesting detail, because after two days of incubation, the eggs would no longer be edible.

Jean postponed his journey to the coconut palms until the next day and returned to Bon Repos in order to find a bag of the string genre, with a mesh that was not very tight, fabricated with his first coconut thread.

As it was, it was perfect. Jean half-filled it with fiber, returned to his deposit of eggs, packaged them carefully, and came back heavily laden. He ate about a ten for his meal, in order to vary his diet agreeably. In spite of their slightly oily taste, the eggs were very digestible.

Until that day he had only eaten raw aliments, although he would have liked to procure fire in order to ameliorate the preparation of his food. He put the rest of his eggs in the coolest part of the cave. Could he conserve them for a few days?

The next day he went to the coconut palms, and on the way back he killed two enormous crabs. The coconut crab, of the genus *Birgus*,[5] attains a monstrous size. It possesses two pairs of pincers; the first, placed on the animal's head, are enormous and can weigh up to three kilos; the others, smaller, replace the last pair of legs. This is how the crab succeeds in nourishing itself of coconuts: after having torn the envelope fiber by fiber, al-

_____

[5] This genus is native to the Indian Ocean and the Pacific. As usual, the account given here of its natural history is almost completely mistaken, but that is not entirely Champsaur's fault, as accounts given in the travelers' tales on which he is drawing were usually fanciful.

ways toward the extremity where three little eyes are found, it strikes it in the same hole until and opening is contrived by hammering; turning its enormous and hard pincers toward itself, it then extracts all the white albuminous substance from the nut with the aid of its thin posterior pincers. The Birgus crab spends the day on land and all night in the sea.

Lying on his bed of palms and sand, Jean thought about the new resources that were about to augment and vary his meals. He did not know yet what the four coconut palms would render. He resolved to sacrifice ten nuts in order to augment the number of his palm trees.

He planted a part of each harvest, choosing the terrain carefully, fertilizing it with detritus and his own excrement. As for the turtles, it was sufficient for him to study their habits in order to reap a considerable harvest therefrom. There was also no lack of crabs; encircled by coral reefs, the shore on that coast was covered in vegetable and animal debris: cephalopods, jellyfish and dead fish. In that compost-heap, crabs and lobsters found abundant nourishment.

The most urgent matter was to make fire. Jean had already tried striking two fragment of flint, but he had only succeeded in producing inconsistent sparks. Wood was lacking, so he could not rub together two pieces of wood in the manner of savages. The hero sought another means, but did not find one.

Suddenly, he shivered, in the midst of the profound silence the same damp click that he had heard before was repeated.

CHAPTER VII
The Infernal Tunnel

He listened, with a certain anguish.

The strange noise recommenced in the water. It always came from the depths of the cave. Thus, there had to be water at the end of the tunnel: a natural reservoir sheltered from the solar radiation. That water must never dry up, it could be a great resource for him, since he would not have to travel the three or four kilometers separating him from the well of the river.

At that moment, through a chink at the summit of the cavern, moonlight penetrated all the way to the entrance of the tunnel at the back. Jean got up, armed with his club, and went forward cautiously, testing the ground ahead of him with a strong palm vein. He covered a hundred meters like that; the fissure, filled with the debris of stones mingled with sand, formed an almost flat ground, but the slope became increasingly evident.

The young man increased his caution, and, fearing that the pebbles might roll under his feet and cause him to lose his balance, he advanced slowly, constantly feeling the left-hand wall and tapping the ground in front with his stick. When he stopped, after a certain lapse of time, he judged that he had covered at least two hundred meters. However, he was exhausted, as much by anguish as by fatigue.

To go any further, he thought, *it's absolutely necessary to have light.*

Click! The mysterious sound had just made itself heard again, but this time much nearer. That inexplicable sound had the gift of terrifying him. What living being could produce it? It was not the sound of stones falling in the water. What, then?

He remembered the shadow gliding over the black water of the crater. He recalled the chapter of the novel *The Toilers of the Sea* in which Gilliatt sees passing beneath him, in the magical Caverne des Douves the ignoble form of the octopus, and the idea that the caverns of the island might be inhabited by such monsters caused him as much horror as disgust.[6]

Thus, he resolved to go back rather than confront the unknown in that thick darkness. He turned around and started retracing his steps. Until then he had darted glances behind him from time to time and had seen, like a luminous star, the moonlight illuminating Bon Repos. But, either because the moon, rising into the sky, had ceased to illuminate the cave, or because the tunnel had turned slightly, he could not see anything ahead of him but opaque darkness.

That only augmented his desire to return, and he started climbing the slope as rapidly as possible. In his impatience, he neglected the precautions of the outward journey and nearly slipped on rolling pebbles several times. For more than an hour he hoisted himself up with difficulty. The ground became steeper and steeper, and,

---

[6] Victor Hugo's *Les Travailleurs de la mer* (1866; tr. as *The Toilers of the Sea*) is perhaps the most prestigious of many novels featuring an imaginary species, the giant octopus, and employing it—in the highly unlikely location of the English Channel in this instance—as a monster to be ritually battled and slain.

strangely enough, he no longer felt pebbles rolling beneath his feet. He bent down and felt the ground with his hand; it was rugged in places and as smooth as a mirror in others.

He judged, by touching it, that he was on a lava flow. A shudder ran through him from head to toe. He was not in the same tunnel. He recalled, then, the mistake he had made. In descending, he had felt the wall with his left hand, and in climbing up again he had done the same. Another tunnel, therefore, branched to the left of the first. On the way down he had gone past it without suspecting it, but on the way up by contrast, he had left the good tunnel to his right. Where would this one end up? What should he do? Turn back, or continue the route going forward?

He stopped, and tried to suppress the agitation of his mind and reflect calmly. By going back down he risked leaving the tunnel again and penetrating into another shaft. Since he was on a lava flow, this one must, of necessity, lead toward the summit of the volcano. He therefore resumed walking forwards, always keeping his hand on the wall to his left, while sounding the void in front of him with his stick.

Suddenly, his left hand was no longer touching anything; a new tunnel opened there. Without letting go of the corner he stretched out his right arm, elongated by the stick, and encountered nothing.

What ought he to do? Follow the new tunnel to the left, or risk traversing the old one? A grave initiative to take. By traversing, he risked entering into a new maze from which he might not be able to get out.

On reflection, he judged that the best thing o do was to go upwards, always upwards, ever ready, if he ended up in a cul-de-sac, to retrace his steps.

Without quitting the corner, which was his only guide in order to return, he lay down on the ground and felt the floor of the new gallery; it seemed to him that the slope was steeper in that direction.

He took it, therefore, still groping in the same way, and went a hundred paces like that. Suddenly, his stick no longer encountered anything but a void. Jean threw himself backwards swiftly, then, lying on the ground he advanced, crawling. The terrain terminated abruptly in a sharp ridge. Our hero searched the ground for a pebble in order to sound the depth of the hole, but in vain. Then detaching his club, which he had slung over his shoulder, he threw it. It fell vertically and, without rebounding, touched the ground; then, after a time that seemed to indicate a long trajectory into the depths, rebounded and plunged into water.

It was necessary, then, to have suffered so much only in order to die there like a dog.

He resumed walking, but this time, with a feverish haste, he went up, down, and up again, falling into holes that were fortunately not very deep. He climbed out, resumed walking, sometimes bumping his head on a low ceiling, dragging himself, groping, tumbling, falling and getting up only to fall again.

Finally, exhausted, bloody and hungry, Jean stumbled one last time. His head collided with the rock rudely and he lay there, unconscious.

CHAPTER VII
The Labyrinth of the Volcano

It was a strange sensation that extracted Jean from his unconsciousness and recalled him to life. He put his hand to his shoulder and brought it away again wet. Beneath him the ground was soaked with water, and a veritable stream was flowing beneath his shoulder.

He stretched himself out and dipped his lips in it. The water was slightly warm. Even so, he was able to slake his thirst, which was devouring, and immediately experienced a relief. On reflection, he concluded that it could only be coming from the exterior. A storm must have fallen upon the island and the water, originating from the torrential rain typical of the tropics, was penetrating into the mountain through all the fissures. There was, therefore a hope of salvation for Jean. He had only to go upstream toward the source—which is to say, toward the crevice—and he would get out of the inextricable maze.

In spite of his extreme exhaustion, he set forth again. It was necessary not to lose a minute; the stream might dry up with the rain that had given birth to it. He followed the stream, therefore, paddling in the water in order not to lose the track. It was not an easy thing to do; the path was far from being uniform. Sometimes, the hero encountered water accumulated in hollows; he sometimes traversed them swimming, but it was necessary for him to find the alimentary stream on the other side and follow its course to another pool, scaling blocks of stone, crawling and sliding through narrow passages.

He stopped in order to listen to the sound of a waterfall that was audible a short distance away, and it seemed to him that the darkness was becoming less opaque. Gradually, as he went forward, the light increased.

A few minutes later, he penetrated into a vast cavity, at the summit of which a dazzling beam of light projected all the way to the bottom: a light sufficient to reveal the new cavern.

From the luminous opening, a thin trickle of water was falling vertically into a rather vast basin, the overflow of which was alimenting the stream that had guided Jean. The young man marveled to begin with; the cavern was entirely the work of exterior fires; it was one of numerous chimneys that had given passage to lava, ash and scoria. The opening through which the light was coming was nearly sixty meters above the basin, and the walls, once calcined, disengaged from parts shorn by pluvial erosion, only allowed the sight of jet black granite varnished with bright red, caused by iron oxides. Other oxides had given birth to green, yellow and other hues.

The basin, no longer forming anything but a vast mirror in which the blinding light from the summit was reflected, resembled a lake of fire, of all the colors of the granitic walls. The walls loomed up on every side, radiant and smooth, rendering it impossible to scale.

After a last hope of escape, it was a complete annihilation. Harvez, fallen on the edge of the basin, contemplated stupidly therein the image of a desperate man, in which he had difficulty recognizing himself.

That was the handsome Jean Harvez, that bearded, hirsute being covered in bruises and bleeding, his hair stuck together with mud and pebbles? He had become frightful, and he scared himself.

He contemplated himself for a long time, stunned by that implacable fatality, and succeeded, by dint of repeating the same memories, in no longer even thinking about it.

Suddenly, a start of astonishment, almost of fear, brought him upright; in the liquid mirror, another image than his own was reflected. He turned round slowly. The image was, in fact, there, but less clear than in the water of the reservoir. He therefore leaned over the "Well of Light" again—for he gave it that name subsequently. The apparition was still there, but seemed slowly to be drowned by the darkness.

There, close by, a human form was depicted. A woman crouching, was extending her torso of a goddess toward him; her face, illuminated from above, had an expression of domination and determination, as well as desire.

Yes, it was Her! It was his statue, his Alluring!

Once again, she merited her name, for the artist, panting with joy, was ready to throw himself into the abyss in order to rejoin the mirage.

A flash of reason finally made him understand that he was only seeing a reflection, and again he turned round. Behind him, the fantastic idol was repeated, but she was not at the same angle of reflection relative to his viewpoint, and only presented a vague and crude form to him. What miracle could have produced that strange phenomenon? Oh, a simple cause, like all physical causes, when one has succeeded in reaching the moment of explanation.

Ten meters above the level of the volcanic cross-roads, a sort of narrow crack opened in the calcined wall.

From that issue, for centuries, infiltrations had followed a siliceous terrain, which, by natural combination, forms stalactites and streams, depositing stony masses on the rocks, sometimes affecting bizarre forms. Thus, in certain places, the creations of that singular phenomenon have been give names such as Christ, the Virgin, the elephant, the bear and the lion.

In the cavern of the Well of Light, calcareous substances running through that crack in the granite, had led to the feminine form in which the sculptor Harvez rediscovered the pose and the sketch of his statue. But if the reflections in the central basin gave her a normal stature, in reality the calcareous mass was seven or eight meters high. The statue itself measured a good five meters. Under its feet, the stony stream poured out in picturesque steps to terminate in a basin whose bottom and sides, covered with the same layer of white silica, certainly indicated petrifying qualities.

As the daylight declined in the cave, the statue was reflected more vaguely in the well, melting as if to be lost definitively into the darkness. Soon there was nothing more than his own silhouette still visible, because it was immediately beneath him.. For a long time he remained thus, looking at himself, as if that figure were the last living shadow that he would ever see, and it was the contemplation in question that, by virtue of a rather bizarre fact, finally reminded him of reality, if not of hope.

The sign seemed to draw away from him, to darken, diminish, and diminish further, and finally to disappear. He raised his head again; up above, the luminous ray was climbing toward the edge of the crater. Then he understood. The sun was descending toward the horizon; it was about to cease illuminating the interior of the crater. But that was not the veritable cause of the disappearance of the image; the level of the basin was lowering, slowly but in a continuous fashion. Already, Jean could see appearing, at the level of the water, new galleries into which the water must have flowed, as it had through the one that had brought him, the unfortunate castaway. That was doubtless the last, for all movement stopped at the surface of the lake, and, at the same time, it became the color of lead. Up above, the chimney was only illuminated any longer by the reverberation of the sky. A few more hours and obscurity would come to augment the horror of that mysterious abode.

Should he await the arrival of a new dawn? What would be the point? Tomorrow would be similar, and tomorrow he would be even weaker. What should he do? Retake the route that had brought him, or attempt the adventure of another issue? He was obliged to descend again, since he could not continue to climb. Perhaps he would be fortunate enough, on another path, to encounter an ascendant or lateral tunnel? They existed, since Bon Repos was one. But he could not count on that, for almost all volcanic chimneys have a vertical slope.

Why seek elsewhere? This corridor opened under his feet; he did not even have the leisure any longer to choose another. The shadow was invading the depths of the gulf, and only the lake retained a crepuscular reflection. Already, a few stars were appearing in the water, and it was as if a new sky were being born above him. After a brief hesitation, he let himself slide as far as the opening and plunged into the darkness.

At first the ground was regular enough; then the wanderer stumbled and fell into numerous ravines still full of water. He was still holding on to the wall to his left, with his right hand extended before him. Sometimes it was necessary for him to bend down and walk crouching, or drag himself on his belly with the apprehension of running into the bottom of some impasse and remaining there as if in a coffin of stone. For a long time he struggled desperately, fell, exhausted and somnolent, and then, in a surge of energy, set forth again.

The memory of Nano came to reanimate him in those minutes of agony; he wanted to see her again, the statue, his marvelous image.

"Nano…! Nini…! Niña…!" he cried, and his voice rolled with a terrible sound.

As if the name had the comfort for Jean of a presence, he continued on his way, calling: "Nano…! Nano…!" Echoes sent the name and the face back to him. He walked in a sort of somnambulism, murmuring less and less forcefully the cherished name, which represented his entire past life, his vaguely immortal work, his work of amour.

Fever took possession of him. He experienced vertigo, and then came hallucinations. He suddenly saw a field of daisies, with their hearts offered in the center of fresh white petals. Also white, came The Alluring; she stretched her marble body flexibly. She became roseate, living, in tender flesh. Frightened, Jean extended his bloody arms toward her.

"Nano…! Nano…!"

She did not seem to see him, and, coquettishly, started to pick flowers. She raised herself up, naked and immodest, so desirable, in sly poses. Then, slowly, she pulled the petals of a daisy and her lips moved, seeming to murmur: "Does he love me…? A little…: A lot…?"

"But I adore you!" he cried. "You're the Enigma. How could I believe that I was able to forget you?"

He resumed running toward his vision.

Suddenly, his forehead collided with a rock. He fell backwards suddenly, letting go of the wall, rolled on the stones and, like a whirlwind, plunged into a tunnel. Then there was a fall into a void, with an avalanche of stones. He had the vague intuition that it was the end, swallowed up in the central gulf, inhabited by unknown monsters. For an instant as brief as lightning, he saw his statue again, The Alluring.

Then he lost consciousness.

CHAPTER IX
Fire

When Jean came to, his astonished gaze wandered around and he wondered whether he was not dreaming. He was at home at Bon Repos, in his cavern. Outside, a dazzling sun was sending him its bright light. At the first movement he made, however, he perceived that it was not a bad dream but a very cruel reality. He was literally molded by and almost entirely buried in a mask of sand and pebbles, from which he had great difficulty disengaging himself. He dragged himself as far as his bed; he found the place, but the palms and fiber had disappeared. He was so exhausted by fatigue that he could not drag himself as far as his larder, and scarcely had he lain down on the sand than he fell into a heavy slumber.

When he woke up he felt better. He succeeded in standing up and headed for his provisions—which, fortunately, were intact, thanks to the precaution he had taken of placing them in a high and profound crevice.

On examining the disposition of the place more carefully he understood what had happened to him and to what fortunate circumstance he owed his salvation. The tunnel through which he had so brutally operated his return to Bon Repos was only the prolongation of the one through which he had departed in his exploration. In the beginning, the cave did not exist; the two tunnels were only one. The erosions caused by inundations repeated millions of times had degraded the softest parts of the granite wall, and one day of great deluge, a part of the wall had collapsed outside. The enormous block was the principal section of it.

Thus, by virtue of the torrential tempests that fell upon the island, the water falling from the highest parts of the mountain had inundated, first, the Well of Light—Jean still gave the cave without an issue that name—and had then spread into all the ancient chimneys of the volcano, which probably converged on the central well at a mysterious point. But since the collapse of the wall, the water had found a new outlet; it no longer ran toward the central well but fell directly into the great crevice in which the river ran. If our hero had been asleep at the moment of the inundation he would have been carried away with his bed and hurled from the height of the cavern into the river which, at this moment, must be full—of which he was able to assure himself. It was flowing full tilt and was engulfed impetuously in the defile, too narrow for its delivery; it changed there into a white torrent of foam.

At the moment, exit from Bon Repos was impossible, for the base of the large rock disappeared under the impetuous waves. But Jean was not worried about that, he knew that such floods could not last for long. He therefore set about preparing a meal of which he had great need. He swallowed a few turtle eggs, ate a good portion of dried meat and half a coconut, all washed down with very fresh water collected from a pool in the cavern. The inundation had the advantage for him of allowing him to be better acquainted with the good and bad sides of his domicile, which would permit him to correct them later for the amelioration of his installation.

He had to remain inactive for a further two days in order to recover completely On the third day, shortly before nightfall, he left Bon Repos in order to return to his coconut palms. He was anxious to know how they had supported the tempest. The river, still rather high, permitted him to swim there, and he was in great need of bathing in order to wash away the mud and blood by which he was covered. At the same time, the warm bath did him a great deal of good.

Landing in the good spot, and having climbed the bank, he saw with joy his four coconut palms extending their plumes of verdure proudly toward the sky. Only ten or so nuts, half buried in the sand, indicated that a tempest must have shaken the palm trees forcefully. He hastened to collect them.

As he picked up the last one, he made a singular find, the nature of which he could not explain at first. It was a sort of cylinder about a meter long and much smaller in diameter, composed of aggregated sand agglomerated with a blackish substance similar to glass.

On examining it more closely he ended up understanding what it was. During the storm, lightning must have struck the soil of the island. Doubtless attracted by buried metal, it had created in its trajectory, by virtue of a natural physical law, in the combination of the sand and soda, a kind of coarse glass grained with sand. The entire mass must have weighed about a hundred kilos, so Jean could not carry it away. He contented himself with taking his nuts and then coming back with a stone club in order to break the cylinder.

He had a great hope, and, in fact, he was not mistaken. When he succeeded, with a large pebble, in breaking the block of glass, he found parts inside that had the limpidity of crystal. He took a few pieces back to Bon Repos in order to fashion them at his leisure.

After having chosen them carefully, he broke them into even smaller fragments. Among others, he obtained one that seemed able to fill the office of a lens. During those various preparations the night had gone by. Jean shredded a little fiber carefully, tore up a few palm leaves, gathered a few pieces of palm trees picked up from the bed of the river, and waited, impatiently this time, for the sun to rise.

The star was exactly on time and at its most ardent, more dazzling than ever. The naked man had laid out his various combustibles at the edge of his cavern; he waited for the desiccation to be complete. That did not take long. Then, sheltering himself with two palms that served as a parasol, he took his piece of glass and turned it until he had found the focal point of his crude lens, which he then directed at his fiber.

It caught fire immediately. The wood, and then the large pieces of coconut palms, caught alight thereafter. A lively and bright furnace was soon burning on the rock. Then he slid a dozen eggs under the ashes, and then put a piece of meat between two hot flat stones.

When it was all sufficiently cooked, he crushed the yolk of the eggs in a bowl, pored coconut milk into it and mixed it all up. It was not exquisite, nor very delicate, but for a man who had been living on raw or dried food for twenty days, the meal seemed delicious. The main thing was, above all, that he had fire: the fire with which, finally, he would be able to do many indispensable things.

Lying on his bed, delivering himself to the digestion of a copious meal, he allowed his imagination to take pleasure in all the benefits that he would be able to obtain from his new ally.

The magic word *fire* enabled an entire new era of adventures to shine. Through his closed eyelids he saw the flame and its conquests. He knew that fire existed on

71

the island; he had seen its traces in the fantastic colorations of the well of light. With fire he could make tools and weapons.

He thought for a long time about his new possibilities; then the idea of the apparition of The Alluring surged forth in his thought. With tools, he could remake the statue of old in that magnified, deformed and magnificent sketch; it could watch over him. What did the absence of a woman matter to him, since he could create a form that, animated by the breath of his genius, would content his desires? A frisson of the desirous lover and the voluptuous artist ran through his entire being. After the struggle for existence, the struggle for amour and for art!

Yes, he would create The Alluring again, an image of the beauty that no one could resist, not even its creator. He could already see, standing out from the somber background of the cavern, the white form of the siliceous mass. He would bring her out of the granitic rock entirely, carve her, polish her and create her with his hands. He sensed, already born beneath his hands, the supple and rounded form of the hips, the firm breasts, the appealing arms, the smooth crossed legs, the lips altered by sensuality in the beautiful taut face. For him, it was not even the perfect beauty of woman that he wanted to create any longer; it was the unique Nano, the one to whom he dedicated the tension of his senses, exacerbated by the impotence to embrace.

That vision passed, he returned the reality and drew up a plan for several enterprises appropriate to augment his culinary resources. For, alas, if one wants to live, it is necessary to think first about nourishment.

CHAPTER X
The First Fishing Trip

For a long time he had wanted to eat fish, but he would have had to content himself with raw or dried fish. Now that he was the master of fire, it was a different matter, and he immediately undertook the necessary preparations. He knew that coral reefs are always frequented by numerous swimmers; they find a shelter and a refuge from the large carnivores of the ocean, which cannot follow them there.

For that enterprise, many things would be useful. He set to work immediately. The main thing was the confection of a good line, capable of being able to resist strong adversaries.

He succeeded in that, thanks to the reptile skin, which he fashioned with its own grease; he cut it into thin strips by means of a shard of glass secured between two palm fibers. Then he twisted them carefully. He obtained thus a cord twelve or fifteen meters long, as thick as an ordinary pencil. He would have liked to make it thinner, but it was impossible. He tested its strength by suspending himself from it afterwards. The result was good; it did not break. He attached a hook to the end made from a bone of the same animal, which gave him the most difficulty. An entire day would not have been too long to finish it, and even then he was not certain of its solidity. At the other extremity he placed a palm rib attached at the middle, which permitted him, if necessary, to fix the line between coral branches.

Then he made two small grids, again with palm ribs, which he reinforced by attaching them together to form regular rods about a meter and a half long, united by fifty centimeter crosspieces; it was a kind of ladder, tight enough for the foot to be span two bars at once. That apparatus was necessary in order to be able to advance over the coral without the risk of falling between the branches. He picked up one grid in order to place it in front, as he advanced on the other.

After that, he made a bag with coconut fiber large enough to sling over his back by means of cord braces. With his ax, his glass knife and a club made from a large stone, he was carrying equipment weighing about twenty kilos.

All that work took him four days.

He set forth at dusk. As always, the night was very clear; he had to be ready for moonrise, which occurred about two hours after sunset.

He would not have had too much difficulty reaching the place where he had landed on the island, but this time, instead of traversing the Black Lake, he arrived at the coast via the south-west of the island, passing behind the cliffs. He reached the shore, not at the precise spot where he has set foot on it but a few kilometers to the south. Departing from Bon Repos he turned his back to the river and followed the base of the mountains. He headed toward the sea, across a plain of sand from which enormous blocks of rock emerged in places.

Having disposed all his equipment on the beach, he waited, not for long. The moon rose and illuminated the whole coral reef with its silvery light.

As the tide would rise at the same time as the lunar globe, it was preferable to commence fishing before the star reached its zenith, because the reefs would then be covered by a meter of water. At first our hero advanced over the coral easily. Near the shore, broken branches, mingled with sand, filled in the interstices, making a compact block. Gradually, the coral ring was uniting with the shore, which it would increase further; afterwards, the present ring, entangling debris and sand in its turn, would retain them on its edge, filing in the bed. When it was no more than thirty meters, new polyps would begin to grow there. The island would be increased in size. That game could continue infinitely.

Thousands of centuries of planetary life resemble the seconds of a human life. The island, initially a volcanic cone, would become an Australia, or, at least, an island like Ceylon or Martinique. Who knows whether, thousands of years ago, the volcanoes of Auvergne did not once give birth to the Gallic land in that fashion?[7]

After three hundred meters or so, Jean reached the coralline massif. The spectacle changed. The moon rose, and its oblique rays recomposed the colors of the prism through the branches of living coral, while behind it the rising tide broke in silvery foam against the scarcely-emerged reefs: a marvelous spectacle. Jean, amazed, forgot the goal of his excursion for a while.

The water was so pure that the light penetrated to a depth of ten meters. He admired the coral branches covered in living flowers, shaped into arches and festoons of a fantastic architecture, between which thousands of fish of all forms and colors played.

Finally, the fisherman tore himself away from that magnificent spectacle and the material aspect of the enterprise occupied him entirely. The place he had reached became perilous for, although the top of the reef was

---

[7] Any geologist.

horizontal, the entanglement of the rings did not form a unified surface. It was necessary to ensure one foot and then seek a point of support for the other. Jean extended his grids over the coral, lifting up the fist in order to place it in front of the second, and so on; he advanced slowly, but surely.

After having covered a short distance in that fashion, he ended up finding what he was looking for, an open space in the reef a few meters in diameter where fishing would be possible. It was a sort of lake caused by a depression in the bed; coral cannot grow—or, rather, cannot live—below thirty meters. Sometimes, such holes are not very deep, at other times several hundred meters. That is what permits channels in coral islands through which ships of a considerable tonnage can pass.

Jean approached his two grids to the edge of the little lake and prepared his equipment. Not knowing what he would have to do, he fitted the end of the line, terminated by a crosspiece, between two branches of coral. The hook garnished with a piece of the skin of the marine lizard, he threw his line, weighted with a pebble, into the middle of the circle.

He did not have long to wait. Scarcely was the bait three meters deep than a terrible shock nearly precipitated the poorly-equipped fisherman into the water. Clinging on to the reef with one hand, lying flat on his grids, he let his line pay out, retaining it with his other hand with all his strength, fearing that it might break. Arrived at the limit, it tightened, but thanks to the crosspiece it held firm, and Jean began to bring back his line, releasing it from time to time in order to tire out his prey.

Finally, he saw the head of a superb fish appear at the surface. The young fisherman made one last effort, reached his victim, maintained it, and struck it a treble blow on the head with his club. The animal, stunned, then allowed itself to be dragged n t the grid. There Jean finished it off by breaking its spine.

The he recognized a fish of the genus *Zanelus*,[8] a large and squat fish, yellow on the belly and black on the back. It had two powerful fins disposed near the head in order to give it a great strength of resistance. This one fortunately, was not one of the largest, for the man would not have been able to defeat one of those easily. It only weighed about five kilos; it is not rare for them to attain double that.

Fish of that species are highly esteemed, substantial and delicate in taste. Tempted by that success, Jean disengaged his hook, which had held good, baited his line and threw it again. It was as well that he had secured his crosspiece; a mighty shock snatched the line from his hands and precipitated him into the sea. He regained his grids swiftly, lay down upon them and waited. The line tightened and relaxed incessantly, with terrible shocks. It held firm, and Jean, who had initially regretted not having been able to make it thinner, now congratulated himself. Had it been weaker it would surely have broken.

Suddenly, a monstrous animal, a devil fish, a sort of ray of the shark family,[9] leapt out of the water and fell on to the reef some ten meters from the fisherman. The

---

[8] The genus in question is nowadays rendered as *Zanclus*; *Zanclus cornutus*, the Moorish idol (*tranchoir* in French), the only extant representative of the genus, has vertical stripes and does not resemble the description given of Jean's fish.

[9] The devil fish, or giant devil ray, *Mobula mobular* does not correspond exactly to the description given in the text, not being equipped with the long tail credited to Jean's fish, evidently an unknown member of the genus.

monster measured at least one meter eighty to the birth of its tail, which was nearly five long. Fallen on the surface of the coral, it thrashed madly, whipping the air with its formidable prolongation For more than half an hour the monster attempted to return to its humid abode, but in vain. Having seized his line again, Jean inflicted continual shocks on it, which gradually tore its mouth, and with the loss of blood it weakened gradually. The fisherman did not despair of bringing the contest to a conclusion.

Finally, in a furious effort, the fish jammed its tail in the coral and could not free it again, which reduced it to impotence.

Jean did not reflect on the danger, and threw himself into the water. With a terrible blow of his glass ax he struck the animal at the birth of its tail. The cut was deep; the wounded animal tried to turn round, but, tightly held, it was paralyzed. The young victor redoubled his blows and ended up severing the formidable tail. Thus detached, the animal recommenced its desperate bounds. Jean remained aside until the efforts relented due to blood loss. Approaching then, he stunned the devil fish with blows of his club.

Jean contemplated his victim; it had to weigh at least two hundred kilos. It was in vain that he tried to shift it. Unable to do that, he opened it up in order to take the liver, which weighed at least five kilos; then he detached a few choice morsels of flesh, about twenty kilos, and abandoned the rest. During that last labor the moon had reached its aphelion and the tide was at its highest point. Standing on the reef, the young man had water up to his neck. Not without difficulty, he loaded the product of his fishing and his instruments on to the grids and he swam to the shore, pushing them in front of him. He reached it without too much difficulty, filled his sack, put it on his back, and set forth with his instruments under his arm.

Two hours later he was at Bon Repos. His fire was extinct. He had to wait patiently for sunrise in order to cook, In the meantime, he cut his fish up into thin slices and the prepared the liver, which he wrapped in the skin of the devil fish. That task occupied him until the desired time.

First he buried the liver under the previous day's ashes and made a good fire on top. While it was cooking he laid out the meat in the sun, went down to fetch water, and finally went to table. The meal was succulent.

Afterwards, he lay down on his bed and thought about his various adventures. He decided not to return to the place where he had been fishing. Given that an animal like the devil fish could penetrate it, other animals even more dangerous might be able to enter it. He therefore resolved to search for a smaller basin. In any case, he could not do anything with such large fish.

For the moment, he had enough food for ten days. He resolved to spend six or seven in various tasks and he amused himself by planning the employment of his time:

The first day—or rather, the first night: search for combustibles.

Second night: exploration of the defile,

Third night: various labors.

Fourth night: search for turtle eggs.

Fifth night: plantation of coconut palms and various tasks.

Sixth night: different tasks.

Seventh night: ascension of the volcano.

Afterwards: fishing expeditions, excursions in the island, etc.

That division of more than a week of projects was, alas, interrupted by a catastrophe.

CHAPTER XI
The Turtle Tracks

Already, in the course of his various expeditions, our hero had explored a corner of the island—or the supposed island, since he had not yet been able to determine its exact configuration.

He had acquired the certainty, however, thanks to the line of foam emphasizing the refs, that the latter encircled the part where he had landed and the Black Lake to the west, and all of the visible part of the coast to the south. He knew that a current had carried him as far as the reefs, but he did not know exactly where yet. It was very important for him to discover its location, because it was at the junction of that current and the sea shore that he had the greatest chance of encountering algae, wrack and other marine plants, and perhaps wreckage.

He therefore decided to take the same route again, but, instead of descending, to climb the escarpment that formed the cliffs on the side of the ocean that had barred his path when he arrived on the island. Continuing to baptize his domain he called that place the Trigonioids, the cliffs the Distress, and the place of his first fishing expedition the Devil Coast.

Having arrived at the highest point, his view overlooked the coral reefs entirely, perfectly visible at that moment because it was low tide. The bank appeared to extend as far as fifty kilometers; although Jean was very high, he could not see the end of it. In the direction of the volcano and that of the Distress the thickness of the coral indicated clearly the depth of the sea: to the south-west, thirty meters, to the north-west, a greater depth.

Coral polyps are not born below thirty meters; he therefore estimated that the current must first run westwards and go around the reef—which is to say, draw away from the island—in order to approach it again toward the south. It was therefore in that direction, where the shore was hollowed out to form a little gulf, that it was necessary to head.

The Turtle Plain was an expanse of sand strewn with enormous rocky blocks. Although the coast appeared to him to be rather sinuous, he resolved to follow it all the way to the gulf. From there, a chain of hills departed that extended toward the coconut palms. That way, he could not go astray among the blocks of stone, which were numerous enough to form a labyrinth.

He therefore went down toward the sea and submitted to its capacious undulations. He had been walking for an hour when he came across fresh turtle tracks. He kept a lookout for it, and a little further on he perceived the animal, which was moving slowly toward the interior of the island.

The man thought: *She's looking for a propitious place to lay her eggs.*

And he followed it at a distance, taking great care to avoid being seen. The turtle already knew the propitious place, because it proceeded without hesitation.

Suddenly, another appeared further to the right, and then another. Jean then had the idea of looking behind him. In the distance, several black dots were moving in his direction. Veering to the left, Jean scaled a rock; that way, he could see what was happening.

The first turtle, having finally found the favorable spot, turned around on its axis several times, tracing a deep furrow on in the sand to its right, in which it laid its eggs. Then it repeated the operation in reverse, and remained motionless. Shortly afterwards, the other turtles caught up with it and started repeating the game on their own account. Jean counted nine turtles, which promised him six or seven eggs each, making about sixty, which he promised himself to collect on the return journey. He retraced his steps cautiously, in order not to attract their attention, and resumed his route.

He reached the small gulf, and found there, on the shore, various kinds of wrack and seaweed—in small quantities, but there must have been several tons in total. He set to work immediately, but realized that it would be much harder that he had thought. For want of any implement, he had to pull them up by hand. The marine vegetation was so sticky and slippery that after six hours of very tiring work, he had only brought ashore a hundred kilos. It was necessary to lay them out then, in order that the next day's sun would desiccate them. Then it would be necessary to make bales of them in order to take them to Bon Repos.

He had the opportunity, while working, to observe that the reef only commenced at that place a hundred meters from the coast, which indicated a deep bed, and, in consequence, a kind of interior channel.

As the night was advanced, he began the return journey, and when he encountered the turtle tracks again he followed them in order to go and collect the eggs. The area was undoubtedly much frequented, for he noticed numerous mounds, nests of incubation, but as the others were surely older, he only took those he knew to be that day's. After some time, such eggs are no longer edible only good at the most for furnishing non-comestible oil. He did not care about that.

The harvest was seventy-two eggs. That was too many to conserve fresh, but by cooking them he could utilize them in a hard state and employ them instead of bread, or, by mixing the yolks with coconut milk, make excellent soups.

As he could see the chain of hills leading toward the coconut palms from where he was, he headed in that direction. He had covered a hundred meters when, going around a rock, he found himself face to face with an enormous turtle. It was certainly as astonished as he was, but it did seem overly alarmed, the sight of a man being unknown to the island's inhabitants and the animals being unaware of the dangers of such a proximity.

For him, the encounter was a veritable stroke of luck, for, in addition to its carapace, which would be a precious cooking implement, the meat and oil collected would be inestimably valuable. But what means was there, after having killed it, of transporting an animal that must weigh two or three hundred kilos? He could only take the carapace and a little of the meat, with which he could charge himself.

Suddenly, an idea occurred to him that was so baroque that he burst out laughing; it as the first time he had laughed for more than a month. That did him good mentally. The well-known phrase from Rabelais radiated its verity in his brain: laughter is the human prerogative. He felt lighter, as if rejuvenated.

Jean's idea was to conduct the turtle to Bon Repos and keep it alive there for a time. But what means was there of making such an animal obey?

Meanwhile, the turtle, doubtless weary of being observed, had decided to resume its route toward the sea. Jean struck it on the head with a light blow of his club; immediately, the animal withdrew it into its carapace and no longer moved. That did not suit our hero. He tapped one foot; the turtle veered in the opposite direction. He repeated the operation, and succeeded in turning the animal completely in the desired direction. Now it was necessary to make it walk. He tried to push it, but it would not budge. Jean administered a series of taps with the club to its back, but nothing worked.

Finally, he had another amusing idea. He remembered the crazy way that a dog runs around when a saucepan is attached to its tail. He had a piece of rope in his sack. He tied a large stone to the animal's tail The effect was immediate; after having shifted the tail in order to get rid of the unusual weight, the poor turtle launched itself forward, and soon, increasingly frightened, accelerated its speed. It was not as fast as the trot of a horse, but Jean estimated that it would nevertheless reach the crevice before sunrise.

From time to time, the turtle was tempted to flee toward the sea, but a blow of the club, applied to the right side, put it back on the path.

Soon, our hero, weary of walking, sometimes to the left and sometimes to the right, installed himself, along with his bale, on the back of the animal, which, increasingly frightened, hastened its forward course.

While traveling thus, Jean thought about where he might house his little vehicle. He recalled that the base of the volcano presented numerous fissures; he only had to make the animal enter one of them and cut off the route of retreat by means of large stones.

In fact, he succeeded in doing that. The animal, guided to an opening almost as wide as itself, plunged into it stupidly, withdrew its head into its carapace and did not move again. Jean leapt down, and built a veritable wall of stones behind it. Thus wedged, the turtle became part of the mountain and could no longer detach itself.

When the operation was concluded, the young man climbed up to his home, did his cooking and went to bed.

CHAPTER XII
The Visit to the Defile

When he woke up at about three o'clock, Jean thought about the utility of the previous day's capture. It would not be easy to kill it; the head was protected by the carapace; cutting into it with an ax would destroy the shell, of which he wanted to make a receptacle.

He remembered having read that in the Pagas archipelago[10] the natives, in order to strip turtles, pile ardent firebrands on the back. The heat lifts up the shell, which becomes concave instead of convex; with the aid of a knife, the skin of the animal can then be detached. It appears that it does not die immediately, and vegetates for some time before succumbing.

The means was barbaric, but Jean had no alternative. He therefore resolved to attempt the operation before nightfall. He lit a large fire in order to have ardent embers.

In the meantime, he commenced the exploration of the defile, at least half of which was in shadow. The heat was stifling there, but, not receiving the direct action of the solar radiation, it was bearable.

The defile, which appeared from the cavern to be a long, practicable trench, was not the same seen from below. Enormous blocks of stone obstructed it, which it was necessary to go round incessantly. Fortunately, the two walls were close enough for it to be impossible to go astray.

---

[10] The Philippines

After having gone around some twenty blocks without getting very far, he spotted a kind of ledge few meters above him, which appeared to follow the wall on the side opposite Bon Repos. He searched for a place from which to reach the ledge and saw that one of the blocks he had just gone around approached it very closely. He scaled it quite easily, and the summit was, in fact, only about a meter above. Jean jumped. The ledge was more than two meters wide at that place. It was a long fault of a softer quality than in the epochs when the defile had been transformed into an impetuous torrent. The water had slowly disaggregated the surface, perfectly flat, without a crack or a pebble. Jean congratulated himself on his find and then advanced rapidly. Beneath him, the gorge was has uneven, but the large blocks gradually gave way to smaller ones, mingled with pebbles and sand

He covered three hundred meters like that. Suddenly, the defile and the ledge were cut, and fell steeply into a gulf that appeared to be at least thirty or forty meters deep. At the bottom shone a liquid surface, wrinkled by gentle ripples by virtue of the fall of numerous trickles of water pouring from several places difficult to distinguish.

That well appeared to be about a hundred meters in diameter, and was almost circular. Jean raised his head. The mountain rose up as far as the eye could see, to a vertiginous height. He judged that it must be the principal chimney of the volcano, the one that must form the terminal cone of the mountain. It was the deep in which all the waters falling on the island ended up. The well could, therefore, be an inexhaustible reservoir for him, unless—which was possible—it was in communication with the sea.

He judged that the sun would not take long to disappear. It was necessary to return to Bon Repos before nightfall. Thick darkness must reign in the gorge, which was profoundly enclosed. He therefore put off until another day a more complete exploration.

Thus far, the architecture of the volcano had been revealed to him with increasing clarity. He understood the formation of the island by subterranean forces, its sculpture by the waters and its augmentation by the coral.

The return journey was accomplished much more rapidly than the outward one. The hero did not have to grope any longer; henceforth, he knew the route and could go to the central well in less than an hour.

When he was at Bon Repos, the fire, lighted before leaving, was no more than a heap of ardent embers; but he had not thought of a means of transporting them to the turtle's back. Finally, he solved the problem by heaping up wood and dry algae on the animal's shell; then making a few ardent embers to leap into a coconut shell with the aid of a stick, he set fire to it. Immediately, a bright fire rose up and the turtle emitted a long whistle of distress. Impossible as it was for it to move, it felt itself burning alive.

Jean followed the operation attentively. Under the influence of the heat, the edges of the shell began to rise up, uncovering the skin, rough but susceptible of being cut. Jean took pity on the poor animal's suffering, and as soon as the opening was adequate he removed the ardent embers and attacked the animal at the shoulder.

It was not easy work. His glass knife was not easy to manipulate. The turtle shifted its feet desperately, any encounter with which might have been dangerous. The savage overcame the difficulty by slipping a large stone between the carapace and the shoulder. After an hour of labor, he succeeded in disarticulating and then detaching one limb. He plunged his knife through the opening and reached the animal's heart, finally putting an end to its suffering.

Then he was able to remove the barrier that blocked his victim and commence butchering it properly.

Having detached the carapace, with weighed at least forty kilos, by means of his ax and his knife, he then removed the thick skin, laying bare the flesh and skeleton of the turtle. As he went he disposed everything around him on flat rocks.

As he worked he rejoiced in provisioning himself with all sorts of riches that the unfortunate captive was going to give him, for, in addition to flesh and oil, the skin the shell, the claws and. finally the bones and entrails would all be extremely useful. At the same time he thought that if anyone could see him at that moment, he would not find him very seductive. Hirsute, he was sweating in large droplets, covered with blood and grease, stained by smoke and ash.

In the split carapace, turned upside down, he heaped up all the grease that, meted, would give him a excellent oil. He detached the flesh in order to dry it, and set aside the bones, which would be particularly precious to him.

The sun rose. The work was not completely finished. Jean resisted until the last minute. The cruel bite of the terrible Father of the World was costly, but he regained his abode with the last slice of meat. For want of a larger receptacle he had to cut it up into little pieces, which he boiled separately in coconut shells placed in the middle of embers. It was his first pot-roast, and that natural meat would be a true feast for him. He postponed the meal to the evening and contented himself for the moment with hard eggs and devil fish liver.

Afterwards, while his little pots were simmering, he lay down on his bed of palm fiber and finally savored a well-earned rest.

CHAPTER XIII
Various Labors

When Jean had attributed the next day to "various labors" he had had no suspicion of the new resources that he would have at his disposal. When after having swallowed an excellent consommé and absorbed a large bowl of turtle broth, he made an inventory of his provisions, he truly did not know where to begin.

Under the influence of the solar heat, all the grease had metamorphosed into oil, almost filling the carapace in which he had tried to contain it. He had great need of more receptacles, but on the island, entirely made of rocks, he would not find any soft substance capable of being baked into pottery. He therefore resolved to attempt the adventure with the resources in his possession.

At dusk, he set forth for the turtle gulf. There he collected the marine vegetation that he had laid out, and which a sunny day had desiccated completely. He made it into four bales. He had time to fish for more and he worked until he had amassed a large heap. He laid them out as he had the previous ones; then he filed his bag with shellfish of all kinds: clams, mussels and a species of oyster with an enormous shell, each weighing at least a kilo.

Finally, laden with a back-breaking burden, he returned to his abode. After having lit a large fire he set out his shellfish in the embers, which did not take long to open. He withdrew them as he went along and put them into coconut-shell cups. His empty mollusk shells were thrown into the fire; then it was necessary for him to wait until they were thoroughly charred.

He prepared an original meal. He cooked all the shellfish together, and then composed a sauce with sour coconut milk and crushed hard egg yolks, salted and mixed in such a fashion as to make a thick paste. He set it down on a flat rock, which served him as a table. In the middle of the paste he put all the mollusks and folded the edges over them, which made a sort of pâté, surrounded the whole with palm leaves and buried it under hot ash. Above it, Jean put a few ardent embers, and kept it in the fire until he deemed that it was sufficiently cooked. Finally, he sat down at table at the moment when the sun surged forth over the horizon.

It only remained to congratulate himself on his culinary invention; unfortunately, the ensemble was a trifle dry; he promised himself to render it more unctuous next time by greasing it with coconut butter or turtle oil. He drank, in addition, a good dose of sour milk mixed with water. He planned to make that liquid ferment in order to extract a sort of alcoholic beverage therefrom.

When his meal was over, as he was not yet sleepy, he devoted three hours to the manufacture of tools for which the turtle bones supplied the raw material. Unfortunately, the skeleton of the animal in question does not possess any long bones, the largest are those of the thighs and forearms; those of the feet are strong but very short and can only serve to compose objects of small dimension.

Jean succeeded nevertheless in fabricating two punches and a kind of fork with two teeth, which, fitted with a hilt of palm rib, was a precious implement for the preparation of food. With the slightly concave shoulderblades, he planned to make spatulas and spoons.

Satisfied with his labor, he went to his alcove and went to sleep, dreaming of nothing but future progress.

CHAPTER XIV
The Potter

In order to avoid endless repetitions, it can be taken for granted that, with rare exceptions, the day of the hero of this adventure commences at sunset and concludes shortly after sunrise. Later, when Jean had managed to create a parasol, he sometimes risked confronting the star in daylight; that was not always devoid of danger.

That said, on with the story.

On awakening, the nudist breakfasted on the previous day's leftovers; then he went to his fire, which was extinct but still very hot. He moved aside the embers carefully and exposed his heap of charred mollusk shells, which had conserved their form. As soon as he touched them, they crumbled into dust. Using the shoulder-blades of the turtle as shovels, he withdrew that dust carefully; then, descending to the river, presently dry, he started searching for a little humus. The harvest was meager; it was only in the vicinity of the coconut palms that he found some; undoubtedly it had required many years to create that clayey soil. He scraped the bottom conscientiously and gathered about as hundred kilos of earth in a hollow. Having heaped stones above it in order that it would not be carried away by the current if a storm arrived, he put ten kilos on one of his shoulders and went back up to his workshop. He still had enough combustible material.

First he constructed an oven by means of flat rocks, behind which he heaped up a hood of moist sand in order to maintain them. Having no griddle for his fire, he was forced to substitute for it by forming supports with similar flat stones, set perpendicularly, on which to place his pottery. The inconvenient detail was not being able to seal his kiln, but he judged that, since the baking would be done by day, the sun would make up for that.

That preliminary work took him two thirds of the night. Very little time remained, therefore, to finish his work. He then commenced to mix the clay with the ash of the seashells and a little fine sand, in liaison with water mixed with the albumen of turtle eggs. For more than an hour he kneaded his paste repeatedly; it seemed very pliant. On a tray made of the eternal palms he commenced the construction of a pot. He rolled the clay into a thin cylinder on his flat tray, and then into a spiral. He thus obtained a vase similar to the classic cooking-pot.

When his composition was a few centimeters high he heaped up, combined and smoothed his torus of clay and continued the operation until the vase was capable of containing about ten liters. Concluded, it did not look bad. Jean placed it carefully in the middle of the oven, heaped wood and dried plants around and beneath it. He lit it at the precise moment when the sun surged forth from the waves. He had a hasty meal of dried meat and two hard eggs, and then withdrew into his cave and lay down on his bed, while following the operation with his eyes.

Jean got up from time to time to put fuel on the fire. Finally, he went to sleep. His slumber was agitated and he woke up well before the end of the day. He ran to his oven. The vase was standing up majestically in the middle, but it was impossible to touch it. How could he hasten the cooling? In the meantime, to counter his impatience, Jean returned to the gulf in order to search for combustible material and shellfish. The previous day's fry-up had been to his taste. The night was spent thus, followed by the preparation of pastes, cooking, etc.

After his meal Jean could not wait any longer; his hands and feet clad, Jean penetrated into the oven swiftly, seized the pot and withdrew, half-singed. He had prepared a bed of dry sand on which to place his pot while it was still hot. He could not suppress an oath of disappointment. The vase was perfectly baked, but large cracks striped it in all directions. With a kick, the apprentice potter knocked it to the ground, where it shattered into ten pieces. Jean started to curse and swear frightfully.

When his anger had passed—which did not take long—he picked up one of the pieces. The pottery was beautiful, dark gray in color, and as hard a iron except for the existing cracks. Jean had to hit it hard with a stone to break one of the fragments.

Suddenly, he slapped his forehead. "Triple idiot!" he roared. "Come on, there's nothing to do but start again!"

He did so, with urgency.

The night passed thus, and a part of the morning.

The nudist was so absorbed in his work that he forgot about nourishment and repose. When the star marked midday on his sundial, Jean had completed a pot and a plate. He went to place them in a location warmed by the sun but in shadow, for fear that excessively rapid drying might crack them. Then he boiled in coconuts the cartilaginous parts of the turtle and a little of the abdominal carapace. He thus obtained a very thick glue, with which he coated the interior of a pot and a plate. Then he waited for the next day in order to repeat his attempt at baking.

Three days later he was the possessor of two receptacles, which were very crude but capable of going in the fire. Henceforth certain of success, before continuing his métier of potter, Jean resolved to improve his tools, which took him many days—or rather, nights.

First, he constructed an oven in a fissure near the cavern; he put it together there with the aid of a trellis supplied by the dead coconut palms. That oven, composed of carefully chosen stones linked together by means of his pottery clay, had all the commodities. The fissure was large enough for there to be an area close to the oven for drying, and a kind of ditch for the trituration of the paste. Later, he obtained by means of the fusion of the crude glass, mingled with turtle-shell and certain seashells, a very consistent enamel of a beautiful bronze hue, with which he coated all his pottery. He thus obtained, purely by the effect of chance, enamels of an agreeable color and an astonishing hardness.

At the entrance to Bon Repos, Jean had constructed an oven for cooking. He had placed it within his reach, but far enough away to avoid the heat. That very prosaic aspect of the young mariner's life cost him many hours, and many days, of labor. Incessantly improving his nourishment, it had the advantage of avoiding the ennui of solitude. While working he talked to himself or sang, because, having read several stories of castaways, he knew that, at length, one lost the use of speech and even forgot the familiar language of the civilized, after having devoted a great deal of time to the preservation of material life.

He did not remain inactive; he attempted by means of intellectual exercises, to maintain in progress the knowledge he had acquired previously.

CHAPTER XV
The Secret of the Volcano

The day after his new conquest of pottery, Jean resolved to return to the Central Well. As the route was known to him, he arrived there very rapidly. For more than a fortnight no rain had fallen on the island; the rivers and crevices were completely dry. In these cases of long dryness, the adventurer was obliged to renew his water supplies from the well of the river. Its depth, of several hundred meters, appeared to be inexhaustible.

Having arrived on the edge of the gulf, Jean found the level considerably reduced; no more streams of water were coming from the upper galleries. A sepulchral silence reigned over the abyss. Lying face down, Jean advanced his head over the edge. Bizarrely enough, the light that had come from the top of the volcanic cone previously seemed this time to be rising from the depths of the well. He understood the reason for that easily. At the height of the surface of the subterranean water, on the side of the sea, a kind of vast porch opened, the base of which must be deep underwater, but the summit appeared to be three or four meters above it. Through that large hole the exterior light penetrated into the well.

During the first visit, the liquid swollen by the rainwater and doubtless also by the exterior reservoir had drowned the porch completely, which now emerged, the water level having dropped, and allowed exterior daylight to penetrate. From that luminous stream was born, on the surface of the water, an entire magical world. The vitrified walls of the volcanic chimney were colored with a thousand various shades passing from violet-black through Sienna browns, ochers, crimsons and greens to the tenderest pinks and ultramarine blues streaked with Prussian blues or tinted with gold, as brilliant as cut diamonds.

Jean admired all of it, dazed with wonder. He could certainly have remained there for hours before that dazzling spectacle if he had not been recalled to reality by a stupefying and monstrous apparition: coming from outside, penetrating into the well irradiated by light, a formidable animal that Jean recognized with horror, by virtue of hang read its description in an account of voyages: the giant squid.[11]

This one, whose enormous tentacles were at least six meters long, must have measured twelve meters when deployed. It penetrated into the well slowly, for it was dragging a large swordfish, already vampirized by the mollusk's treble suckers, for it only indicated a residue of life by rare convulsive somersaults.

Like other cephalopods, the greater part of the squid is soft; a single bone, as in the cuttlefish, forms the skeleton, along with a few cartilaginous portions, and one horny item, the beak, formed like that of a parrot. The squid rips up and absorbs its prey. Unlike the octopus,

---

[11] Most previous writers of adventure stories had employed the terms *poulpe* or *pieuvre*, both of which usually mean "octopus," to depict their imaginary giant cephalopods, but Champsaur is forthright in naming his *le calmar géant*, which refers unambiguously to the giant squid *Architeuthis*, described in various French accounts of natural history since the 1860s, but still a semi-mythical creature in 1931. As usual, Champsaur's account of the natural history of the species is erroneous, actual giant squids being deep sea creatures.

with only has a mouth-anus, the squid has two openings: an entrance and an exit. In the order of cephalopods it is the most complete. The octopus and the cuttlefish are only small sketches of that masterpiece of ugliness. On each side of the beak are two enormous eyes, glaucous and vitreous, devoid of radiation; the head is round poorly poised on an articulation joining the head to the abdomen and the tail. To either side of the beak and above it, ten soft and vigorous arms are welded, each of which has a hundred suckers. No viscera, no sinews, one bone—only one—and no muscles; in those animals the envelope, or rather the skin, replaces almost all the organs. The strength of this one, the mere sight of which terrified the gentleman, had to be considerable, since it could capture and bring back to its lair prey the size of the swordfish. It was tearing it apart now.

When the first moment of horror had passed, the instinct of the hunter resumed its rights. The surface of the water was sixty meters below him. The place where the voracious creature had paused in order to tear apart its prey did not appear to be out of range. He picked up a stone, and with an energetic impulsion, he launched it at the squid. By a fortunate chance, the animal was raising its head above the surface at that moment. The stone struck the center of one of the enormous eyes, and crushed it.

Rendered furious by that wound, the cephalopod released the swordfish and started beating the surface of the water furiously with its gigantic tentacles.

Jean understood, then, the provenance of the noise that he could hear in his cavern, the extremity of the tunnel of which must end in this well. He raised his head and searched the wall of the gulf to discover whether he could see that opening. He did, in fact, see one, ten meters above him to his right. Was that the one? On scrutinizing the walls attentively, however, he discovered three more, one other above, on the opposite side, and two below. He concluded that it must be one of the latter, for the tunnels situated above must be illuminated slightly, and his own was in complete obscurity.

Now that he was the master of fire, Jean promised himself that he would make torches or a lamp and resume his exploration. As for the question of drinkable water, it was resolved. The well certainly communicated with the Black Lake, and the latter with the sea, since the squid came from that direction.

At that moment, his attention was recalled to the depths of the gulf by an unexpected noise. Until then the furious whiplashes of the wounded squid's tentacles had not ceased, but suddenly, the clicking was multiplied tenfold, and Jean, looking again, was amazed. Near the luminous porch there was a swarm of tentacles. There was no longer only one monster but a host. It was impossible, in that swarm, to count them. The young man estimated that there must be at least twenty squid to form that frightful spectacle.

Were the monsters fighting one another, or had the fury of the wounded individual overtaken them? In the depths of the gulf there was a vertiginous agitation. The whiplashes of the tentacles, reverberated by the echoes of the colossal cylinder, made detonations like firearms. Jean, dazed and sickened by the hideous scene, beat a precipitate retreat in order to regain his dwelling.

He finally knew the mystery of the volcano. He shuddered to think that, during his arrival on the island, it was doubtless one of those monsters that had tried to reach him. For him, that danger would always be menacing. He forbade himself any more excursions at sea.

Apart from the reefs, where the animals could not slither, the entire littoral was their empire. How could that hideous and painful proximity be avoided? Perhaps the configuration of the island would furnish the means. For that, it was necessary to know what it was.

Jean resolved to resume further excursions as soon as possible. He ended his day, as usual, with the preparation of a meal, and went to bed, satisfied in his curiosity by having discovered the mysterious inhabitants of the drowned abysms of the volcano.

CHAPTER XVI
A New Maze

A fortnight went by after the vision of the squid; Jean thought about it incessantly, entirely devoted to it during that time of interior labor: the construction of pottery, the fabrication of a few tools, including a large pair of wooden pincers destined to pull various items out of the fires; a few clubs with palm-vein handles; and for weapons, two javelins, for which the large bones of the turtle furnished points, and a bow, made with two strong ribs bound together in the middle, the string of which and the attachments were made with the intestines of the turtle, washed and curried with oil and then twisted into cords. He obtained ten meters of strong string that way, very uniform and very solid, destined to replace the fishing line that was too thick. He also made several hooks with bones, more resistant and better fabricated than the first.

He had not, in any case, returned to the reefs since the discovery of the squid, fearing that he might encounter them in the sea.

That day, having almost concluded his most pressing tasks, he resolved to make an ascension of the volcano. For the moment, the moon was full; it rose three hours after sunset, which assured him of at least six hours of bright light. He therefore went off out the crevice, headed north and descended toward the cliffs. It was in that direction that the volcano appeared to him to be most accessible. In fact, after having gone around the base of the cone, he saw a kind of ridge caused by a lava flow; it was unscalable itself, but on its edges the charred rock had crumbled by virtue of the action of time to form the bed of a torrent, the waters of which, during great storms, must flow all the way to the river.

Jean followed that path easily. The pebbles that had obstructed it at first had been borne away long ago. In places, the path was almost sheer, at others it continued for hundreds of meters at a slope of scarcely twenty degrees.

After an hour of ascension, Jean turned round. He had arrived at a culminating point from which he could embrace a large area of terrain. He judged at first that he was about two-thirds of the way up the central cone and three hundred meters above the crevice. He saw below him the tortuous line of the lava flow glittering in the moonlight like a metal serpent, jet black, in which broad red stripes indicated, once again, the presence of metallic veins.

There was iron so close a hand! What luck!

As far as the eye could see, all the details of the landscape appeared to him with a surprising clarity. The air was so pure, so limpid, that he could see the sea clearly, to the south, the west and the north-west, scintillating under the radiance of Phoebe. Come on! There was no more doubt about it; he really was on a island: Harvez Island. He baptized it with his own name.

On the other side of the volcano, toward the Black Lake, it was also the sea that extended. He could see the entire west and north-west part. The southern part was masked by an enormous rock and the north was behind him.

The conformation of the island was almost that of a fish; its open mouth was the Black Lake. From the base of the volcano, high hills radiated. He already knew some of them: the cliffs and the hills limiting the plain of the turtles, from the gulf to the river. Further to the west, another chain formed a semi-circle, and, rising progressively, went to fall sheerly at the extreme, a little above the well, to terminate similarly over a gulf seemingly much greater than that of the turtles.

At that moment the moon was almost directly overhead; the tide was rising over the reefs, which were covered in foam, allowing their extent to be measured. They departed from the Black Lake all along the coast to the extreme point, at which they turned around it. The west coast was completely free, which indicated great depth.

Having studied hard and retained what he saw, he turned round in order to continue his ascent. Behind the block that indicated the north and the west, the lava flow bifurcated to the north side. It appeared to head, going around the mountain, toward the Black Lake—which is to say, to the east, and then the crevice. Jean followed that direction. Perhaps he would find a more direct and rapid route to return home. The bed of the torrent, running alongside the lava flow, became steeper. At a turning, the young man emerged on to a kind of platform. He moved on to it very cautiously, the ground was deeply ravined.

Suddenly, he recoiled abruptly. Almost under his feet, an abyss opened up, or, rather, one of the ancient chimneys of the volcano. Lying face down, he reached the edge of the gulf and looked down. At that moment the moon was just at the zenith. The first thing that Jean saw was a second moon reflected beneath him. He did not have to make any great expense of imagination to recognize it. He was above the Well of Light. The level of the well had dropped since Jean had ventured into it.

Doubtless the bottom formed a bowl and retained enough water to justify the name that the young man had given to it. Thus he was seeing again the place where he had agonized and thought that he might find death. He recognized all the details, and the same tunnel entrance through which he had fallen, so involuntarily, into Bon Repos.

Opposite loomed up the white mass of the siliceous flow that formed, so bizarrely, the statue of Nano, of Nini, of The Alluring, the *niña*. Seen from above, the aspect was no longer the same, and it required all the fantasy of a lover and an artist to rediscover the trace of a human form.

But the imagination of Harvez had no limits; in the formless mass he saw designed the dominant Nano, the incarnation of feminine beauty. Pensively, he contemplated it. The light moved over the siliceous flow; the moon, instead of being reflected vertically in the basin of the Well of Light, plunged its rays obliquely, and the liquid mirror reflected the image of the Alluring, who took on, regarded thus a more real form. It was from almost the same angle that Jean had seen her the first time. The impression upon him was such that he made a forward movement and almost fell into the abyss.

The instinct of self-preservation made him throw himself backwards. In his brain there was a rapid vertigo, wherein there passed, with a cinematic celerity, his years of work, of compositions. His amour, which he wanted to be dead, in order not to trouble his solitude, reborn, lay in wait for him, in his virility exacerbated by an obligatory continence as well as in his needs of an artist and a creator.

By means of a superhuman effort, he finally tore himself away from that obsession, recoiled cautiously and returned to the bed of the torrent. This time, the lava flow really departed from the central cone and the ascension became increasingly difficult. Finally, he came to a vertical wall and was obliged to stop there, the terminal point of the crater being no more than thirty meters above his head.

He therefore retraced his steps. Having arrived at the platform again, he had the idea of going around the side of the mountain—which is to say, to the east. In that direction, there were no lava flows, and enormous rocky blocks, piled upon one another, sometimes left strange corridors between them through which it was possible to slide. As those hazardous stone pathways appeared to terminate in the vicinity of the crevice, Jean went that way, promising himself that he would not lose sight of the volcanic cone.

Scarcely had he surpassed a few rocks than their mass closed the horizon. He understood the danger and tried to retrace his steps, but all the rocks resembled one another sufficiently for him to be unable to distinguish one from another. As he had descended into a labyrinth he thought that by climbing upwards again he would find the volcanic cone, but he ran into a vertical block that closed the route. He retraced his steps and looked for another issue.

Another dead end.

For two hours he wandered in that chaos of rocks. He began to feel the same anguish as in his excursion in the interior tunnels. At least he could see clearly this time, but the situation was as inextricable. Weary of his many futile efforts, he resumed the descent; twenty times he was obliged to go back, excessively large blocks barring his passage.

Finally, the rocks ended and he found himself on the mountainside. To his left, a slight projection permitted him a point of support, but in order to reach it, it was necessary to risk himself on the slope, which appeared terribly scabrous. Finally, he reached it, and rested momentarily; it was the trench of a crevice that headed toward the base of the cone, going around it to the east. Jean resumed his march. He was often obliged to climb over blocks, arrested in their fall by the fissure, which he rediscovered on the other side.

Suddenly, at a turning, he saw the course of the river beneath him, and a few hundred meters of the path took him almost directly above Bon Repos.

Throughout the danger he had run, he had not taken account of the time or the variation of the light. When he had quit the platform he had still been illuminated by the moon. Then, only the stars had scintillated, and now, the sun was rising.

Beneath him the wall overhanging Bon Repos was sheer. He followed the projection where he was, hoping to see a way down, but it continued at the same height; meanwhile, the wall was as smooth as a mirror. Soon, he was obliged to stop; the heat became intolerable and the burning rocks rendered the continuation of his search impossible. It was necessary to find a shelter.

Thus exposed, stark naked, to the tropical sun's rays, he was assured of a terrible death.

He remembered having climbed over a sufficiently large block; its mass would give him a little shade. He therefore went back and huddled under the rock. On examining the other side of the crevice he was entirely convinced that he was directly above Bon Repos. Advancing his head, he recognized the monolith that he climbed in order to reach his abode. To have his refuge, his bed and his meal so close at hand, and to be nailed to these burning rocks without any hope of getting out of them! He would be too exhausted by twenty-four hours of fasting and fatigue to retrace the route he had followed during the next night.

Oh well! It was necessary to wait for dusk and tempt fortune in the direction of the central well.

That day was frightful. In spite of the improvised shelter, the blinding reverberations of the nearby rocks burned his eyes through his closed eyelids. The disposition of his refuge prevented him from turning his back on the defile. Thirst, more than hunger, made him suffer. Oh, a tempest would certainly have been welcome at that moment, even if it bore him away into the crevice!

Finally, the night so much desired arrived, but alas, what an effort it required for Jean to emerge from his stony covert! However, it was absolutely necessary to find an issue before the return of daylight. Painfully, therefore, he resumed the course he had followed through the crevice, often leaning over the edge with the intense hope of finding a way that would permit him to descend. But it was in vain that he plunged ever deeper into the defile; beneath him, the wall was always as sheer.

There was no more doubt; the ledge was prolonged all the way to the central point, which it must turn around. Was this, then, the denouement? Was he destined to serve as fodder for the monsters of the volcano? He would prefer to go back and throw himself head first into the defile, to be crushed by the fall.

At that moment, as if to double the horror of the situation, the frightful splash of the whip in the water became audible at the bottom of the well.

Jean let himself fall on the edge of the gulf and remained there for a long time, as if deprived of consciousness. It was again the horrible sound that brought him back to himself. At that moment, as on the previous day, the moon, having arrived at the summit of its course, appeared in the orifice of the crater and poured torrents of silver light into the abyss. Mechanically, the young man continued with his eyes the ledge on which he found himself. Brightly illuminated, it was easy to follow its meanders inside the well.

Suddenly, Jean stood up, astounded, and rubbed his eyes. Had he seen accurately, or was it an imaginary creation?

He made a zigzag tour of the well. The first time, the ledge, at a more elevated level than the interior of the crater, had led him to the central well. A singular labor, but very natural. In the epoch of great inundations, the torrential movement of turbulent waters had eroded the softer vein of the originals terrain everywhere. Lifted up by the interior fires, it had ended up outside at a higher level than inside the crater.

It was still a hard proof to undergo. That walk above the abyss of the squid could not fail to impress the naked young man forcefully. He had no choice. He had to attempt the adventure or await death in that place. It was also necessary to take advantage of the moonlight. Fortunately, in its course, the star had to traverse the volcano precisely at its greatest diameter, which promised nearly an hour of light.

Jean set forth courageously. A first, his stiff limbs rendered walking painful, but with movement his pace became firmer and he advanced rapidly. It was not, in sum, a very long journey. He scarcely had three or four hundred meters to cross. The ledge was sufficiently uniform almost everywhere, apart from a few fissures, the largest of which was no more than a meter, which he jumped over without too much effort.

Finally, the circuit was complete; but there was a new disappointment; at the point where the two ledges ought to have met they were separated by a wide gap and one was placed three or four meters above the other. Jean hesitated momentarily; it was a terrible leap to make, but salvation was at the end.

He gathered all his strength and leapt. If the leap failed, he would fall into the gulf.

He landed on the extremity of the edge.

With a supreme effort, he launched his body forwards and fell, rudely, on the edge of the defile. His head hit the ground so violently that he remained there, stunned, for a long time before recovering his senses. He sat up painfully and made an effort to get up, but in vain; one of his legs refused him service. He perceived that the left leg was broken below the knee. He had collided badly with the angle of the ledge and the tibia had not resisted. Furthermore, he had a wound in his forehead from which blood was flowing in such quantity that it blinded him.

He set his back against the wall and waited for a little order to return to his ideas.

A hero ought not to hesitate for long before acting. He congratulated himself, at that moment, for having reunited the ledge to Bon Repos by a bridge made of two coconut palms united in the middle by cords. Without that circumstance he would not have been able to return home, and he would have died in the defile. He therefore set forth, dragging himself, crawling on three paws. Fortunately, the violence of the impact had numbed the broken limb. The pain was considerable, but bearable. He hastened as much as possible; he knew that when fever took possession of him, he would be forced to stop.

It took him two hours to arrive.

His first act was to drink; then he ate two eggs and, refreshed, attended to his leg. He cut splints from his providential palm ribs. After having put the fractured bone in place, not without atrocious pain, he surrounded it with six of the splints, which he found tightly with his new line. As soon as he had done that he felt somewhat relieved, and lay down on his bed.

He did not take long to go to sleep. His weary thought ceased confusedly to be haunted by the memory of the gray and harsh landscapes of the rugged, impassive and ferocious island, without a single flower, butterfly or bird, devoid of wings, women and amour.

And with all the material cares, a heavy virility, more energetic and firmer every day.

CHAPTER XVII
Convalescence

There was, alas, a forced repose. He could not quit Bon Repos, without danger, for a month, perhaps forty days, depending on the rapidity of the suture. He took an inventory of his provisions, divided them into forty equal parts and resolved only to have one meal per day. The hardest thing would be to procure enough to drink. Fortunately, he had filled his large vase, containing ten liters of sour milk and water. He had intended to allow it to ferment in order to make a beverage, and perhaps, eventually, alcohol. In addition, he had six coconuts whose milk was drinkable. As for water, he only had about two liters.

Fever began to devour him. It was necessary for him to make a terrible effort of will to refrain from drinking in accordance with his thirst. Fortunately, after three days the fever disappeared and he was able to draw what remained of the coconut fiber close to his bed, in order to distract himself. With the patience of prisoners or invalids, he started spinning it with more care than he had previously done. He had a good quantity, so he was able to occupy himself with that for two weeks.

His leg was getting better; he was able to move around his cave backwards, in a sitting position. He inspected his provisions. They were still in a good state, but as he had eaten those susceptible to spoiling first, he was reduced to dried meat, not very refreshing for a invalid.

On the fifteenth day, the heat suddenly became stifling, although the young man had retired to the utmost depths of his lair. A burning wind reached him, making him sweat as if in a steam-bath. Suddenly, the light disappeared and he found himself almost in darkness. For the first time during his sojourn on the island he was about to witness a tempest that promised to be fantastic.

He picked up, as quickly as he could, the various objects in the floor and put them in shelter in the crevice of provisions. The he heaped up the leaves of his bed above the most elevated part, and awaited events.

He did not have long to wait. A fulgurant flash of lightning was followed immediately by a formidable crash. The thunderbolt had just struck the defile, the echoes of which repeated the detonation at least ten times. From then on there was an uninterrupted din; the thunderclaps and their repercussions no longer stopped. A deluge fell with such violence that the mountain seemed to tremble. In less than half an hour the river filled up and poured its foaming and furious torrent into the defile. A little later, the tunnel through which the hero of this story had reentered so brutally began to pour a veritable cataract into the cave. Thanks to the barrage that Jean had built, however, the greater part of it was drawn into the depths, where it was engulfed furiously. Nevertheless, the flood was such that some overflowed the barrage and fell into the defile.

That was fortunate, finally permitting him to drink his fill. His thirst slaked, he filled all his receptacles and returned to his niche.

How long did the tempest last? He could not take accurate account of it; he estimated that it was at least two full days. When the light finally returned, the sun was already low on the horizon.

He dragged himself to the entrance of the cave and looked into the defile. The crevice was transformed into the most impetuous torrent, swollen at the entry point into seething foam, the water rolling stones detached from the mountain. They piled up at the entrance to the long corridor, obstructing it and further increasing the violence of the current.

That chaos, in which all the unleashed elements seemed to be delivering a battle of savage and terrible grandeur, was an impressive spectacle. The last solar rays plunged into that liquid turbulence slantwise, the light decomposing there into all the colors of the prism, while up above, little rainbows formed and disappeared incessantly. Marveling, Jean stayed there contemplating the spectacle until nightfall put an end to it. He returned to his bed and went to sleep, wondering whether his co-conut palms could have resisted a hurricane of such violence.

The next day, everything had returned to its habitual order. The defile emptied progressively, but the river was still full. An ardent sunlight, penetrating into the cavern to a depth of three meters from the entrance, gave Jean the idea of making himself a little broth. He therefore sacrificed some of his palm-ribs to light a small fire, which he then transported to his oven. He had some difficulty dragging and lifting up his pot full of water, but, pushing and pulling, he finally lifted it up above his head and succeeded in sliding it on to the oven. Then, for the first time he stood up on his valid leg and made a little excursion, hopping, around his domain. He attached a reinforcement to the end of his bow with a rib, and thus obtained a staff strong enough to support him without buckling.

From then on, with the advantage of verticality, he was able to attend to his cooking more easily. A few hours later he digested an excellent broth, the restorative benefit of which he felt immediately.

He eked out his provision of water, which ran out at the same time as his fracture healed. He contained his impatience to walk until the fortieth day, because he knew that excessive haste might be fatal. From the thirtieth day onwards he dragged himself around progressively. When the term of his reestablishment arrived, he was almost as solid as before.

That was another hard proof through which he had passed.

In spite of his firm determination to resist the power of memory during his long hours of forced immobility, and above all during the mechanical work of spinning the fiber, he had been unable to prevent his wandering mind making frequent backward returns. The desire to complete the work sketched by nature eventually came to persecute him incessantly.

Why not? The dream was realizable. He had fire; he had the certainty of finding iron on the island. He occupied his long insomnias thinking about means to extract that iron. The paradox of his situation was that he needed the metal to make tools, and needed tools to extract the metal; for he could not hope to attack the rock with his mass of glass or stone. Even if he had to scrape with his fingernails, he would extract the particles necessary to make a hammer, and then...

Then he saw himself attacking the calcareous rock and correcting the sketch in the Well of Light. But to return to that subterranean crossroads? Bah! This time he had fire, which is to say, light. He would make candles with coconut butter, or better still, in order to get there more rapidly, he would use the route taken to return to Bon Repos. He would be able to construct a ladder or a kind of staircase by piling up stones; however difficult it might be, all his determination would be directed toward that result: seeing The Alluring again, recreating her, more beautiful and more tempting, even better realized than his first conception.

And he suddenly remembered his first sculpture, which he had fashioned in a candle at the age of twelve: a young woman respiring a pink rose. The child had colored the flower.

When he was able to go out, he began by making a visit to his coconut palms, which he found in a good state, except that ten nuts lay half-buried the sand; it was an excellent fashion of having an obligatory harvest before the due date. Jean collected them in great haste. He saw that the ten nuts he had planted had germinated and were growing above ground with stems already thirty centimeters high.

"In a few years I'll have fourteen coconut palms. I'll plant twenty; that will make a fine palm grove, and progressively, I'll increase my domain." He was not unaware that it required seven or eight years for that palm tree to bear fruits. That did not enable him to make dreams of leaving the island.

Ballasted by his nuts he headed toward the plain of turtles with the hope of capturing one, but it was in vain that he searched the area. He explored several mounds that appeared to be nests of eggs, but while he was ill the eggs had hatched and the young turtles had returned the sea.

That gave him the idea of going toward the shore. It was as well that he did, for he encountered ten of them on the sand. Although they were in their first month of existence they already weighed nearly a kilo. He killed four and, satisfied with his first excursion, he returned to Bon Repos.

One of his baby turtles provided a meal by way of a roast; the others, skinned, were cooked in a pot where, under a layer of grease, they waited to be eaten in their turn. In his brain, at that moment, the beast was dominant rather than the unquiet cares of existence: the mere need to live vegetatively for a while.

CHAPTER XVIII
A New Excursion

Jean's last adventure had put him off the mountain; he resolved to undertake a reconnaissance to the western point of the island. As there was still sufficient water, he decided to make the journey swimming all the way to the source. The strange river was, in sum, only a long and narrow reservoir. He thus attained, without fatigue, the chain of hills that extended in the form of a crescent from the plain of the coconut palms to the tip of the island; but the barrier of a small mountain was so steep at the point that he was obliged to follow the base, veering toward the south-west. That brought him closer to the southern coast.

Postponing scaling it until another day, he reached the edge of the sea. In that direction the shore, which was entirely rocky, stopped abruptly, at a height of two or three meters. Having nothing to obtain from that disposition of the terrain, he was about to beat a retreat when the idea came to him of climbing a big rock in order to study that part of the island a little more carefully.

That was a fortunate thought. From that post he saw the coast elevating gradually until the horn of a small gulf. Another chain of hills appeared to originate near the well of the river and came to fall into the sea from a height of at least thirty meters.

As the ascension of those hills seemed fairly easy, Jean made a tour of the gulf, which was no more than two kilometers in diameter. He climbed the hill without much difficulty; on the other side it descended in a gentle slope to the sea. There was a hollow; as far as the eye could see the shore was cluttered with masses of wrack and other algae.

"That's an inexhaustible provision of combustible material for me," he said, "and I'll have the river to transport it by harvest time. The difficult thing is building a raft."

While making those reflections, Jean had descended to the shore. Then he saw that with the coastal seaweed, half or three-quarters buried in the sand, there was a quantity of wreckage, stuck together by the oceanic vegetation with preserves and shellfish.

In order to comprehend that abnormality, Jean had to reach the extreme point of the gulf; then he was able to explain the creation of that marine cemetery easily, by the disposition of the coastline. The current that had brought him to the island went around the coat along the coral reef; then, turning southwards, ran into the hollow, where, necessarily, it left everything that it had ferried in its journey, heading thereafter directly southwards, to disappear in mid-ocean.

"Well," said the castaway, continuing his monologue, "There a current that might furnish me with the means to signify my presence here."

In the meantime and in order not to lose the habit of action, he set to work immediately.

He went into the water waist-deep and undertook the disengagement of a large piece of wood, but it was not an easy task. The ligneous fragment, half-embedded in the sand and almost completely covered in shellfish, was very heavy. It was first necessary to free it from the sand, work that our mariner had to do by hand, with the sole aid of a large flat seashell that served him both as a scraper to clear the sand from it and as a shovel to throw the sand further away. Finally, with heavy blows of a club, he cleared away all the shellfish and wrack that weighed upon the wreckage.

After two hours of dogged toil, he succeeded in dragging to the shore half of a yardarm snapped in the middle. It was made of two pieces of wood combined by two iron collars maintained by pins riveted to the two sides. Pulling, pushing and rolling, Jean succeeded in bringing his conquest to dry land, on to which he threw it. Now, nothing was simpler than to return to his dwelling swimming, pushing the piece of wood in front of him.

While working, he had noticed that the entire mass of debris and vegetation was swarming with marine vermin: crabs, lobsters, crayfish, mussels, oysters, sea-urchins, shellfish of a thousand species, octopodes of all kinds and jellyfish, all mingled together, dead and alive, devouring one another. There was an embarrassment of choice, so he disdained the small fry in order to capture and kill six crayfish and two lobsters, all of a respectable size, of a total weight of at least twenty kilos. That was, for Jean, a good night's work, which would restock his larder. He returned to his abode swimming, pushing the yardarm and the produce of his hunt in front of him, his heart full of joy and satisfaction.

CHAPTER XIX
The Gulf of Wreckage

The next day, at sunset, the hero set forth for the Gulf of Wreckage. The discovery made the day before incited him to further research. This time he was equipped with his longest ropes and a large sack, one of his most recent achievements. When he reached his destination, the ocean, at low tide, had left dry a good third of the surface of the gulf and all of the south-eastern coast of the island. There, the shelf had to extend a long way into the sea, for the tide and withdrawn more than ten kilometers. He made that estimate because, from the height of the promontory at the point of the gulf, as far as the eye could see, he could no longer see water mirroring the stars.

He descended to the shore. He had the advantage, if he made a find, of not having a cliff to climb. The route was far from being easy; the entire shoreline, apart from a few long tongues of sand, was entirely covered by a dense layer of seaweed of every species, and it would have require special tools to drain that marine compost-heap. He advanced for some distance into that chaos of vegetation, examining each large accumulation carefully.

He had already searched a few heaps without finding anything but worm-eaten pieces of wood that crumbled in his hands. To one piece of wreckage, a strong iron ring was attached, from which hung a chain some two meters long. He had no great difficulty in detaching the metal; the end literally fell apart.

Having carried away the ring and chain he was more fortunate, a large mass of wrack attracted his attention. He ran to it and, tearing away the weed, laid bare the keel of a launch, the rim of which was entirely buried in the sand.

He set to work, and after three hours of dogged labor he succeeded in disengaging the boat and turning it over. It was a small disembarkation launch, which two oarsmen were sufficient to propel. Apart from a large rip in the bottom, it seemed still to be in good condition.

With the particular skill of an artist, Jean succeeded, by means of tightly wadded wrack, in blocking the inconvenient opening. While waiting for the tide to come in, he continued his research. He collected a few pieces of wood in good enough condition to carry to the shore. He left a few on the shore that seemed appropriate to repair his launch. In the meantime, the moon had commenced its habitual course on the horizon. The tide rose with it, and the mariner, who had returned to the launch, already had water up to his knees. Half an hour later, the boat was afloat.

Jean blocked a few slight infiltrations, then leapt into the vessel, with the end of a plank to use as a paddle. He succeeded, not without difficulty. All the weed returned to the surface with the tide, and hindered him considerably. By following the tongue of sand, however, sometimes sculling and sometimes leaping into the sea and pushing the boat in front of him, he reached the shore and pulled the launch on to the sand.

He took an inventory of his find, and saw with joy that a few pieces of plank were garnished with nails; he had eleven in all. Without pincers to extract them, however, he had no other resource than burning the wood in order to obtain those precious objects. After reflection, therefore, he threw all his planks into the river, having bound the lot together with his cord, and, pushing that new raft, he went back to his lair.

It was necessary for him to put off the repair of the launch until the next day, for the wood had to dry out first. He therefore laid it out outside, and lit his fire. Shortly afterwards, he threw the chain and the ring on to the incandescent embers, as well as the two iron rings of the yardarm, which he succeeded in disengaging by expelling the pins. In order to achieve that the ingenious engineer had to wear away the side of the rivet and then expel it with one of his bone punches. Fortunately, the wood, dried beforehand in the sun, did not adhere to the metal, so he was able to carry it through, but it required half a day's labor. He had put the two pins to one side, preciously. They were about twenty centimeters long, as thick as a little finger; he intended to transform them later into tools or weapons.

Soon, all his scrap metal was red hot.

Then an obstacle presented itself about which he had not thought; he would have needed a fire-rake to shift and soften the metal, and he did not have anything. He was looking around desperately when his eyes encountered the two pieces of the yard-arm, which, thus doubled, resembled a long cylinder divided in two. Making use of the sharpened end, it was roughly manipulable, on condition of moistening it incessantly. He put his largest receptacle, the shell of the large turtle, near the fire. All things considered, that went better than he hoped. Every time he saw that the wood was about to catch fire, he withdrew it swiftly and plunged it in the water.

Finally, the operation was concluded to his satisfaction; he obtained a lump of iron as big as his head, pulled it out of the fire, pushed it on to a large flat stone and started to forge it. It was difficult work, for Vulcan was naked, and it was not accomplished without a few burns.

Sweating blood and water, half-cooked, he nevertheless obtained three pieces of iron that, taken up repeatedly and fashioned, gave him after four entire days of labor a pick-ax, a spade and a hammer, all rather crude but capable of fulfilling the function that the forger expected of them.

Before commencing that work, Jean, having returned to the Gulf of Wreckage, had sought and found a refuge for the launch in a fissure in the cliff. He had buried it in a thick layer of wrack. Without that precaution, under the influence of the heat, his boat would have come apart. This time, he was equipped with a few tools, and if he found more metal debris, he would be better equipped to work it.

The hero had take care, every day, to place a small stone in a hole in the cave; on his two hundredth day on the island he was the possessor of a perfectly usable launch sheltered in a little grotto situated on the shore, a kilometer at the most from Bon Repos. It was protected from the sea by a reef bordering the north-eastern coast of the island, which Jean had not yet explored, although he counted on doing so soon. In that grotto, which the tide penetrated completely, the boat was completely sheltered from the sun, and carefully maintained in perfect condition; from the two fragments of the yard-arm the owner had fabricated two solid oars.

Working as a blacksmith, his arsenal had been augmented by an ax, a long rod that served as a fire-rake, a pair of pincers, another hammer, stronger than the first, a spearhead, arrows, a large and sturdy knife—all of a piece, hilt and blade—which he wore at his waist in a turtle-leather belt.

He had obtained that leather by softening the carapace of a turtle in warm water and then pounding it in its own grease; that produced leather nearly two centimeters thick, which he split in order to make strips. With it he also fabricated sandals fixed with thongs. It was not with the first turtle captured that Jean did all that; he had caught killed ten more since.

He finally had the most essential tools, and he was rich in provisions that were not very varied but, being cooked henceforth, became more substantial or more agreeable aliments. He had a pot, well salted, and, under a thick layer of grease or oil, conserves of turtle, crayfish and various fish. He went fishing with his boat. All that was combined with freshly-laid turtle eggs. As for coconuts, they were exhausted; it was necessary to wait for the new harvest, which was imminent; his four coconut palm each bore about the thirty nuts, which were growing well.

CHAPTER XX
The Alluring

Thus, tranquil from the viewpoint of nourishment, he was able to take up his artistic dream again, and take measures to realize it. After having forged a sculptor's mallet and two chisels, he manufactured long candles with dry, twisted wrack soaked in fish-oil, thickened and hardened by the sun. In each of those torches, at the center, for want of a wick, there was a void, produced by courtesy of a strong thread of turtle-gut, which he withdrew when the candle was dry.

He lit one of them in order to ascertain its properties of illumination. Its light was quite bright, and a sixty-centimeter torch lasted for about two hours. There was one inconvenience: the candles ran copiously; it was necessary to manufacture iron pincers of a sort in order to be able to carry them without being burned. He prepared ten torches thus, and took away half of them; then, after having equipped himself with charcoal intended to make reference marks, he set forth boldly into the tunnel that had once nearly been so fatal to him.

Well-illuminated, he had to difficulty finding the various tunnels that were an indecipherable labyrinth in the dark. He explored them tranquilly, giving them different names. The tunnel descending toward the central well, the slope of the squid, was called The Street of the Aquarium of Monsters; the branch to the left, which had led him astray was marked Error Street; the tunnel leading to the well into which he had thrown his club became Distress Street. Finally, the one leading to the Well of Light, the longest and most uneven, now completely dry, was The Street of Foolish Hope.

He reached the Well of Light in less than three hours; he had therefore only burned one and a half torches. His heart was beating rapidly as he penetrated into the cavern for he was about to see The Alluring again. Would the impression be as vivid as the first time?

His two visions had nearly cost him his life; but this time, armed and equipped with the necessary equipment, he went around the Well of Light. At the summit of the cavern, the sky, scintillating with stars, illuminated the chimney with a pale light, for the moon would not make the marvelous sanctuary a paradise that night.

Jean's sensual emotion had calmed down; for the moment, there was only the joy of the artist. He approached the siliceous block and examined it attentively. At close range the statue took on harsh shadows, which caused its details to stand out even more. Its height was about five meters; the mass of stalagmites on which it was crouched in the Oriental fashion was about two. The work would be long and difficult.

At the base, the flow of the calcareous waters had created a basin that retained a rather large quantity of water. By its slightly milky appearance, Harvez judged that it must contain a considerable quantity of calcium chloride, with all the qualities of petrifying springs. In order to make sure of that, he detached a piece of stone with a hammer-blow, which he threw into the basin. But in order to get on with the job he needed a scaffold, and his resources of wood were too minimal. The conclusion was that he could only work by day, his light-source being not very manipulable.

After having examined the different points at which he could attack the statue, he decided on the following dispositions:

To make holes in the granitic wall in which he could plunge pieces of wood; to put strong nails with broad heads into them to which he could fix cords; on those cords to install a kind of platform on which he could set to work. There being no possible recoil, it would be necessary for him to sculpt by judgment, and only look at the effect obtained at long intervals.

In spite of that, and even by reason of the difficulties to be overcome, he decided not to delay for an hour. It was necessary, for a start, to gain time—which is to say, to avoid the long journey through the labyrinth by utilizing the same return tunnel every time. He had brought ropes, which he threw into it. Having lit a third torch, he took stock of the most practical means. The descent was easy enough, thanks to the projections and the form of the tunnel, the entrance to which advanced slightly over the well.

He therefore fixed a rope firmly, equipped with little wooden crosspieces providing handholds, which rendered the ascension sufficiently convenient. Subsequently, he improved it and made it a veritable rope ladder with wooden rungs.

That established, he went down the tunnel, called Safe Return Street, to the cavern. The route was easy, the last storm having cleared away the stones and little pebbles. Only a thin layer of sand carpeted the ground, rendering walking even easier and less hard on the feet. The tunnel was not long; Jean could reach his studio in less than a quarter of an hour. Furthermore, he would have the precious advantage of having water at his discretion, the Well of Light never drying out.

Having arrived at the extremity of the tunnel he fixed a new nail solidly; then attached a rope garnished, like the first, with crosspieces, and descended tranquilly into his home.

In order not to have to return continually to an enterprise that would take the artist months, it is necessary to be content to indicate the means by which Jean could undertake a gigantic task that anyone else would have judged impossible.

He had no lack of iron; thanks to that metal, the sculptor was able to install the singular scaffold that he had conceived. That preliminary work require about three months. He did not do it consecutively, of course, and it was mingled with various adventures.

First, it was necessary for him to make holes in the granite wall outside the siliceous mass, fitted with tampons in order to fix the nails destined to retain the ropes—the fabrication of the ropes alone required three more months. This was the method of fabrication, because his coconut fiber would have been insufficient: he chose carefully the wrack that had great tenacity; he crushed it and softened it in warm water mixed with grease and fine ash, which gave it a great flexibility and rendered it unbreakable. That concluded, he made a métier of rope-making. in which, winding ten threads together meticulously, he obtained ropes twenty-five meters long, the solidity of which he tested by suspending large stones with them, twice his own weight.

In order to make holes in the granite, he had been obliged to wedge into it in advance iron bars more than forty centimeters long, which made a sort of iron ladder with which to attain the height of the statue. He extended from the height of the head the first ropes carrying the platform on which he would stand, and that platform was pulled backwards by two ropes that kept it at a suitable distance from the stone to be sculpted. In order to reach that little scaffold, Jean made use of another point of support extended above his head. It was necessary that the whole ensemble was exactly measured and equilibrated, that the platform should be solidly set and would not swing. Various annexed ropes completed the assembly.

Still by means of the rungs planted in the wall, he succeeded in reaching the crevice from which the calcareous spring ran. Equipped with a torch, he penetrated into it and was able to contemplate a new marvel. That opening, which looked like a mere crack from below, was, in reality, two meters wide. A few steps from the entrance, the wall rose up gradually to form the vault of a colossal cavern. Stalactites fell, joining up in places with stalagmites that seemed to emerge from the ground, forming imposing columns. All of it was a dazzling white. The cavern had a great extent, for Harvez, after having advanced for some distance, could not see the end. Fearing to get lost in another maze, he returned to his point of departure. Thanks to numerous stalagmites that ornamented the floor there was an embarrassment of choice of one to which to attach his rope. He thus had a precious point of support with which to ensure the solidity of his construction.

Six months, to the day, after commencing the work of scaffolding, he took his place on the moving platform and began to rough-hew the statue constructed by the hazards of nature, giving the first strokes of the chisel to the woman of stone: The Alluring.

CHAPTER XXI
The North-Eastern Coast of the Island

The naked young man, although content with the new conquests that he had resolved, did not yet know the full extent of his island. He therefore resolved to continue the exploration, and to visit the north-east one fine night.

He only knew the Gulf of Wreckage and a little of the vicinity. He went there first; from there he would be able to see the land extending northwards, and would be able to return to Bon Repos.

Well-equipped this time, well-shod and equipped with his knife, his spear and his bow, he had decided, if he encountered any animal, to engage it in mortal combat. After going along the shore for half a hour he found himself confronted by two masses of rock forming islets. The smaller one, not far from the shore, ought to be accessible on foot at low tide; the second, the larger of the two, was not very distant from the first, and a little further from the coast. Jean promised himself to study them on another day, and continued his excursion. They were the two Iron Islands.

Beyond that location, the ground rose all the way to a chain of hills going, toward the west, there to join the river, and terminating toward the east in a sheer cape extending into the sea.

Having reached the summit of a promontory, his gaze embraced the entire coast, from the Gulf of Wreckage to the north-west to the volcano to the north-east.

Almost everywhere, the island was similarly surrounded by refs.

Shortly thereafter the moon rose, climbing behind the reefs and illuminating all their details as well as the expanse of transparent water between them and the coast. It was a veritably magical spectacle. On the steep edges of the coast, limiting the sea almost vertically, long strands of seaweed of every sort had grown, forming a kind of thick green velvet fur on the rocks.

Among those weeds, chasing one another, playing and obtaining their nourishment there, an entire band of amblyrhynchi was moving with an astonishing grace and rapidity. As much as the animal is heavy and clumsy on land, in the water, although that element seems inappropriate to serve as a shelter for a lizard, it is supple and rapid. Thus was explained the presence of the island of the first amblyrhynchus he had encountered; that one, too adventurous and too curious, must have gone astray and finally sought a refuge from the sunlight under the debris of the fallen coconut palms felled by the tempest. Jean had been fortunate to take possession of one in order to stock his larder, but it was necessary not to count on killing one as long as they did not return to land.[12]

In the meantime, he continued his exploration by following the shore, always northwards. He headed toward a rather steep point forming a little cape. He reached it after a good hour's march, climbed it, and there had a view of the region between that cape and the

---

[12] In fact, marine iguanas cannot stay in the water for long, because even tropical oceanic water is too cool to sustain exothermic animals for long submarine excursions; they would, therefore, be easy prey.

volcano, where the Black Lake was. He baptized it Cape Amblyrhynch in memory of the saurian iguanids

The belt of reefs extended, joining up with those of the opposite coast; thus, the island was surrounded, with the exception of the part where the current penetrated into the Bay of Wreckage, opposed to their formation, On that coast there was a hollow extending nearly a kilometer out to sea and thus forming a wide channel in which, except in the epoch of high tides, a complete calm must reign, which suited the way of life of the amblyrhynchi perfectly.

Jean therefore knew, at present, almost all of his domain; it only remained for him to explore the eastern part of the island. Renouncing for that day taking possession of one of the giant lizards, he decided to return to Bon Repos and to traverse the valley between the cape and the volcano.

That area, harsh and rugged, was entirely closed by corridors of lava and debris of various sorts. On the way, Jean picked up several large pieces of pumice stone and scoria slightly veined with red, which appeared to him to be held together by iron oxide. In a fissure in the ground he also found beautiful sulfur crystals; thus, the mineral realm was about to take its place among the objects gathered in his house.

The next day he set fire to his finds and collected nearly a kilo of excellent iron. Decidedly, the precious metal was not rare, and he would soon see in his possession a very complete set of tools.

Those multiple tasks were a necessary distraction to enable him to forget his sad situation. For nearly two years, isolated from the world, he had been acutely aware of a void within him, and solitary thoughts; he had to react at all costs in order not to go mad.

In order to struggle more intensely against those weaknesses, he decided to start writing a journal and to relate there everything that he attempted and every interesting event.

That journal and his artistic labor were more than was required to conserve his intellect in a good condition. But for that, Jean had to create paper, or something capable of replacing it; it was then that he returned to his parchment composed of various materials. Having tried fish-skin and the ventral shell of a turtle, he decided to make use of the skin of amblyrhynchi.

That skin, well softened and then degreased with a lye of ashes, and carefully rubbed with pumice stone thereafter, gave him sheets with a surface area of about one meter forty, folded in half or in four. It was thick but supple, and a beautiful greenish white in color. He made pens with bones and ink with soot mingled with a light solution of fish-glue.

He decided to commence his journal of the first day of the third year of his sojourn on the island. He counted the pebbles in his money-box. He had another twenty days to go; he devoted them to the perfection of his installation.

In three years numerous storms had come to trouble the apathetic life of the island, so Jean had gradually metamorphosed the cavern.

He had hollowed out a vast cistern under the orifice of the upper gallery where the water accumulated, thus giving him a reserve that he hastened to utilize after each storm. From the cistern to the orifice of the tunnel below he dug a channel sufficient to take the overflow.

This was now the conformation of the cave. Firstly, it was connected to the large access rock by a solid footbridge made with wood collected from the Gulf of Wreckage.

A solid ladder permitted him to climb the rock without fatigue. In the morning Jean pulled up his ladder in order to use it at home. That had the advantage of permitting him to reach the upper gallery, which he had carefully cleared and rid of sand and pebbles, which would have accumulated and soiled his cistern; that accommodation of the tunnel also permitted him to attain the Well of Light, where he was always certain of finding water.

The floor of the cave, safe henceforth from flooding, had been smoothed out and covered by fine sand. A ledge two meters wide, carved with the pick, put Bon Repos in communication with the furnace, the kitchen and the pottery kiln, situated, as we have said, on a platform outside the cavern.

For furniture there was a table, a bench, a stool and, along the straightest wall, a large set of shelves on which Jean arranged his daily provisions and his tools.

He had discovered in the superior gallery a vast cavern perfectly secure from flooding, and which, by virtue of its disposition, permitted him to make a storeroom for alimentary reserves. A temperature well below that of Bon Repos reigned there at all times, and that was very advantageous for the conservation of provisions.

To drink, eat and love! Is that all of life, then? And yet, for him, life was contained entirely in the first two terms. Love whom? No one! There was no other human being on that lost island.

He only had his memories of the beauty of woman, and, in the entrails of that mound of earth where evil fate had thrown him, a colossal idol, still crude. But for him, she represented *the kiss*.[13]

---

[13] The word *baiser* [kiss] is frequently used in French as a euphemism for sexual intercourse; its emphasis here implies strongly that it is being used in that way in this instance.

CHAPTER XXII
The Flight of Days

Two years had passed thus

To sustain him, Jean had had the conviction that he would get away from the place. He had succeeded in vanquishing hard and cruel proofs. He was there, healthy, his flesh and muscles hardened and fortified to the point of having acquired an uncommon strength.

All his endeavors had obtained good results. There was only one to which he was awaiting a response. He had put coconuts into the current that went alongside the island containing a document indicating his presence. Unfortunately, the impossibility in which he was of making an exact calculation of the latitude and the longitude doubtless left too large a field of research.

While awaiting his deliverance he wanted to undertake an excursion in the ocean,[14] and he risked the adventure one evening, well equipped against the sun that would attack him the following day. He believed that the expedition would be difficult, but without too much danger. It was a cruel error; when he returned he was bruised by terrible suffering.

Equipped with weapons, well shod, clad in his apron, his palm-leaf hat, his legs gaitered in turtle leath-

---

[14] I have translated the original faithfully at this point, although there is probably a mistake, as the oceanic excursion on which Jean embark in a later chapter seems to be his first, and it is from the overland expedition to the north-east of the island from which he returns imminently in bad shape..

er, with a large cutlass at his side, an ax, six meters of rope, a sack of provisions and two coconuts destined to be filled when he quit the river, he believed that he had foreseen everything.

His equipment placed on a little raft made for that purpose, he had pushed it in front of him swimming up-river; he was soon at the extremity; after a long search he found a cliff that permitted him to reach the shore. With his equipment hoisted on to his shoulder he reached the summit of the hill masking the horizon easily. From there, he could see all of the western part of the island.

The hill, of which he occupied one of the culminating points, was about three hundred meters. At the point where he was, it went straight down toward the sea, to the left; on the other, its height was maintained until the extreme end of the island, which it terminated in a sharp point extending northwards, thus forming a vast gulf, which he subsequently baptized Coral Gulf. It was completely closed by reefs; between the coast and the coral bank there ought to be a hollow like the one in the northeast, but much more extensive.

As the tip of the island seemed to Jean to be interesting to observe, he set out for it. It was a very difficult enterprise. At the formation of the island that part must have been lifted up by the interior fires. Everywhere that the rocky crust did not pierce the soil it was fine sand, certainly an ancient sea bed. That sand, overheated and desiccated by the tropical sun, was extremely friable, and wherever the ground offered a slight slope it was difficult to stand upright.

The night advanced and it was time to seek a shelter in order to stay there during the day, but thus far he had seen nothing propitious. He was beginning to be anxious, for the prospect of spending twelve hours under the sun was not at all pleasant. As he had seen nothing since he had climbed the hill, he advanced westwards.

He reached a place where the coast was hollowed out, forming a little bay. He thought at first that there was a chance of finding a shelter there and he set about descending the hill.

Engaged on a sort of rocky ridge, he thought he had a solid point of support in order to descend, but it ended abruptly, plunging into the sand. The bay was only a hundred meters away. He lay down and started crawling toward it.

He was advancing in that direction when he suddenly found himself confronted by an enormous hole that barred his way.

At that moment, the sun rose

That hole must have been one of the first volcanic cones, and the bay was another, which, like the Black Lake, had crumbled into the sea. That disposition of the location promised nothing worthwhile. However, he had some chance of finding a shelter in the direction of the ocean, and he decided to attempt the adventure. He therefore set out to go around the hole, still crawling. He had covered two thirds of the way when his knees slipped and he fell flat.

He made a violent effort to get up, which had no other result than to shift the load that he was carrying, which dragged him toward the gaping hole behind him. He clung on in vain, plunging his arms up to the elbows into the moving sand. He was sliding slowly but inexorably toward the abyss.

By means of a final effort, he turned over on to his back, holding on with all his tensed body. It was futile; a few seconds later he felt himself slipping into the void.

The fall was not violent, and he was buried waist deep in the fine sand, from which he had difficulty freeing himself. He finally succeeded in doing that and was able to scan with his eyes the place where he was. That was not very complicated.

The ancient volcanic chimney had gradually been filled in by the sand surrounding it. Perhaps in a century or two, it would be at ground level. The man judged that he ought not to wait that long, and made a careful tour of it in order to find a means of reaching the orifice. The wall rose up vertically on all sides, without the slightest crack.

Exhausted by fatigue, he lay down on the side that was in shadow, and after a frugal meal taken from the luggage that had fallen with him, he went to sleep.

The bite of the sun woke him up. Then he made a more scrupulous examination of his prison, in order to see what he might attempt the following night. After having made a tour of his cave twice he returned to a place where a sort of greenish flow cut through the dark maroon of the chimney. Jean tested the substance with his knife and found it less hard than the vitrified mass surrounding it. The vein was about fifty or sixty centimeters thick, and seemed to rise all the way up to the opening of the chimney: doubtless the ancient bed lifted up and torn by the volcano.

It was the sole chance of salvation. It was necessary to excavate the fault, hollow out a passage therein and gradually rise up as far as the surface of the ground. He did not wait for dusk, but set to work immediately. Fortunately, he had his knife and his ax.

Night fell and he found himself in darkness at first. Then gradually, his eyes adapted to the gloom, and toward midnight the moon rose, illuminating obliquely the wall on which he was working.

When daylight appeared he had dug into the fault over an extent of some two meters. He had quit the bottom of the well and commenced to climb, carving out steps, in order to have a solid point of support underfoot.

He had made an inventory of his provisions and envisaged, with anguish, their excessively rapid diminution. He had brought food for two days from Bon Repos, assuming that he would be back sooner than that. He estimated, from the work that he had done in twenty hours, that he would need a hundred hours—five days—in order to get out of that prison. He only had nourishment for four days, and for drinking, the contents of one coconut. It was necessary, at all costs, to reduce the rations further, but reducing his aliments was also to reduce his strength.

After a rest he set to work again.

Five days went by, of relentless labor. He was approaching the summit less rapidly than he had supposed

In fact, seen from below, the perspective had caused him to make an error, and he had at least four more meters to carve in the stone. He had eaten nothing for two days and had nothing to drink for four. His strength was diminishing rapidly and at times he had a desire to lie down and cease struggling.

One day more; Jean stiffened himself, but his strength was at an end and his ax and his knife, worn away almost completely, had difficulty digging into the stone.

At sunrise on the sixth day of captivity, he remained lying in the fault without having the strength to go back down. He was scarcely a meter from the goal! How long could he remain almost devoid of consciousness?

A sensation of freshness reanimated him.

He had scarcely opened his eyes when a blinding light made him close them again, and a diluvian rain streamed into his prison. It was certainly the most frightful of all the tempests that had fallen upon the island while Jean had been there. Soon he saw, with alarm, that the chimney of the former crater was, like the well of the squid, the natural reservoir of that part of the island. Lower down than the hill, all the water shed on its flanks came to plunge into that abyss. In spite of its large dimension, the immense well was filling rapidly. Given the torrents of water that were pouring into it, it would be filled in less than four hours.

As one of those torrents was flowing over his head, he only had to hold out his cupped hand to draw from it and drink from the hollow thus fired. For several days he had deceived his hunger by gnawing his turtle leather leggings, but thirst had tortured him more. That providential water was, therefore, a great reinforcement. He resumed contact with life, and was then able to envisage his situation.

The cyclone was increasing its intensity; the flashes of lightning succeeded one another with unusual rapidity; by their intense light Jean saw the water rising at a ever-increasing velocity. A few more minutes and it would reach him. What might have caused his doom was about to save him; he had only to let himself go and sustain himself in the water until it reached the rim of the well, and throw himself on to the slope of the hill.

That was, in fact, what happened. When the water was no more than twenty centimeters from the orifice of the well, he hoisted himself up and obtained a foothold, resistant to the wind and the torrents that barred his way at every step.

144

Finally, the tempest gradually calmed down, and Jean reached the crest of the hill. When it ended and the sky cleared, the stars were shining again. That brought the duration of his expedition to ten days. He retraced the route he had traveled in departure in the inverse direction, and reached the river soon enough to get back to his house before daybreak.

The defile leading to Bon Repos was full to the brim. Jean threw himself in the water and allowed it to carry him to the crevice. There, thanks to his ladder, he was soon at home. He ran to his intact larder. Needless to say, he did honor to its contents.

But he had had enough, he thought as he lay down on his bed of coconut foliage, of the arid, monotonous and melancholy island where destiny had cast him away; the mass of volcanic rock where he now had a diabolical appearance; a lamentable heap of rock and sand, not even cheered up by a fluttering flag: that unknown isle, so unvaried and sad, amid the eternal groaning of the waves of the South Atlantic Ocean.

CHAPTER XXIII
The Call for Help

To every good man, to whom the possibility might be permitted to come to the aid of an unfortunate castaway.

Twenty-eight months ago, Jean Harvez, artist sculptor, passenger aboard the transatlantic liner España, *departed from Rio de Janeiro, destination Bordeaux (France), torpedoed by a German submarine, ran aground by a miracle on a island not very far from the place of the shipwreck, which I believe to be situated on the equator, for I have the sun at its zenith every day.*

I can still live for a long time. I beg you, whoever you are, to come to my aid.

This island is surrounded by coral reefs and is only approachable from the south, where a current passes by to which I am confiding this apparatus and this document, with a little map of the island.

Jean Harvez.

CHAPTER XXIV
The Alluring

In spite of the desperate tone of that appeal for help, Jean was not yet determined to depart.

He did not see the possibility of abandoning his incomplete statue. Jean was habituated to consider the island as being created for her and for him. Having vanquished all obstacles, he was vanquished in his turn by an image, a symbol: the old obsession took hold of him again.

Facing that siliceous block, he discovers, in that body formed by nature, surprising sources of visual and sensual pleasure, all the richness of femininity, all the beauty of perfect nudity. She is imposing, smooth, white, only darkened by an efflorescence of moss blossoming in light filaments, like hair, at the location of the pubis.

He had almost thought that he had invented and created The Alluring, but he saw that she was natural, in order to mock his impotent pride. It was the victory of the unknown magician who perhaps regulates earthly forces.

Jean had set to work, exaggerating the idea of his Nano, in order to make sense of his thoughts, his days and the world. The pagan serenity of amour penetrated him to the point of giving him a corporeal wellbeing that took away the idea of nourishing himself.

Nano was his moral defeat.

He works, lavishes himself, and no longer seeks any other joys now than those given to him by his artistic sensibility.

The anxious pleasure of the conception of ideal forms, the desire for the realization, holds Jean avid, maddened by a tragic thirst. The further his work advances, the more The Alluring makes imperious demands, by which her face, her upper body and her limbs aspire to an absolute plasticity.

He files, chisels, causes stone to fly away in thin shards, in order that Nano, emerging from her painful birth with all the amplitude of her reconquered beauty, can recompense him for his efforts.

He is recommencing the adventure, mingled even more intimately with his creation. Less originality, more reality. He is no longer inventing, he is reexperiencing, with his own breath, the emotion that once cradled his vibrant and voluptuous body.

Imagination no longer ornaments the reality. It is sufficient for Jean's memory to mark a point of arrest in his existence for an essentially dramatic adventure.

He was no longer the fantasist sculptor, the laborious inventor, but the master, life itself, guiding its rough draft to perfection.

Jean was giving the sketch a thrust of wings.

Turned toward that goal, dominated by his creative will, Harvez saw days passing by, one after another, without enchantment, between him and his creation. One might have thought that an exchange of fluids was taking place.

The eyebrows raised high above the imploring eyes, the chin willful, the enigmatic smile suspended from the sensual lips, the curls of the hair falling heavily on to the neck: that is the head. The phantom of curved lines pursues Harvez in the rounded grace of the lowered arms, the joined hands, the very simple fingers, assuring a divine triangle. There is the bust, with the firm breasts, the color of alabaster, the bust, so feminine, thrust forward, the stature refined by the movement, the hips in which the smooth loins are nested, and in the hollow, the siliceous bush of secret charms. The thighs imitate the form of a squatting Buddha; the rounded knees protrude slightly, the feet seem expertly modeled.

Over the surface of the water where her image is reflected, the statue surges, in splendid nudity. Simultaneously taking and refusing, consenting and dominating, she says: "I am Beauty, the immortal work that is worth every sacrifice. In me reside physical and mental sensualities.

"To me belong your intelligence that has seen me, your art that has created me, your will that wanted me thus and your soul, which animates me.

"My power surpasses that of living statues stifled by clothing and convention. Repose your burning head in my lap, man; my hands have only to move slightly to caress your weary brow.

"I am the idol that is adored, not the slave who serves her master on her knees."

Jean sensed in confrontation with his work the same impotent fury that had gripped him before. She was his, entirely, but more Idol than the other, for this one was overwhelming by virtue of her imposing height. Jean could sit down comfortably in the nest formed by her parted knees

He ran his trembling fingers over the firm and beautiful curves of his creature, recognizing all the contours and charming corners kneaded amorously. He recommenced suffering madly from his desire.

149

Jean stepped back in order to enjoy a view of the ensemble and then started to appeal:

"Nano! Nano! My love... Come, Nano...! Come, Nini...! Come, *niña*..."

The entire litany of charming and tender words that one lavishes on the beloved...he had difficulty finding those words again, in repeating the slow labor of the reconstruction of sentences. He applied himself, as much in order not to forget human speech, to making long speeches to his statue, which seemed to quiver under the play of the light. He made the vowels sing and struck the consonants to the rhythm of the words. His voice became firmer, strong and ostentatious. He spoke in English, in French and in Spanish, and saw that he had lost none of his intelligence.

How poor and narrow in space all those people seemed to him who lived in cities and nations, amalgamated! Were they still fighting one another? Could people, yes or no, respire in peace? A mystery! Jean Harvez might never know the outcome of the war that had snatched him from contemporary life.

Every artist lives in a kind of duel between himself and his creation. Nano hung on to Jean, pursuing him, even far away from her, and threw his supreme memory toward Bon Repos, near to slumber and meals.

Gradually, he lost the impetus in the impulsion of movements that had permitted him to live his three years of incessant struggle. He was held by what he held, a slave, where he had been the master.

He went to sit down on a natural pedestal on the other side of the lake and there, naked, a potent statue of masculine vitality, he remained, in a bold pose of Michelangelo and Rodin in rut, contemplating The Alluring.

He looked down on her. She seemed small, and extended her offered face toward him; he saw the image reflected in the lake with growling waters. That insinuating, soothing noise eventually numbed his sensibility, to the point of self-forgetfulness. He saw Nano rise from her frame, come to him, to press herself against his burning flesh, and allow herself to lavish, and him to return, equally ardent caresses.

CHAPTER XXV
Sculpted Desire

In order to attain her more fully, and since she could not come to life, he resolved to sculpt his own body, upright, facing her, with the long spur of rock where he suddenly saw a man, beside himself, gripping his penis. Thus he would await the Idol, the woman, in her habitual pose, and their two reflections, led toward one another by the agitation of the water, would mingle in an embrace.

With all the impetuosity of his being, without sparing his strength, a lover who does not hesitate, he gave himself to his ardent work without reserve. Two months later, the statue of a male with hands in offering, his face turned toward The Alluring, loomed up, whole and part. In fact, the reflections were confounded in the water, as in the caress, in a back-and-forth movement. Jean watched those liquid and diaphanous beings; the sight of them excited, appeased and renewed the thirst that he had for femininity.

He sensed an elevation above himself, made of all his savings of sentimental force, accumulated for too long. Finally, delivered, they spurted in exalted phrases and appeals that Jean launched more and more frequently to the two motionless beings contemplating one another and kissing.

The man felt himself going mad.

He wanted to escape his obsession by means of a great objective. He decided to destroy the squid. He made his preparations for combat and departed.

CHAPTER XXVI
The War Against the Monsters

Having, to begin with, observed the opening of the cavern and the central chimney of the volcano, he had three means of arriving there: the crevice, the tunnel to Bon Repos, and the Black Lake.

He took the most practical: the opening connecting the Black Lake with the central well, about four meters broad and three high. It was constantly immersed at high tide, and when the water was at its lowest level it was almost clear. On the seaward side, the wall was very uneven, but on the side of the well it was as smooth as a mirror. It was, therefore, a matter of sealing that opening when all the squid were in their domicile. Having observed them many times, he was sure that they hunted by night and returned before sunrise. The problem was not complicated, but the sole means within Jean's power required rather long preparations. He needed a grille, of such a fashion that he could place it, so to speak, instantaneously.

He therefore made numerous voyages in his launch to the Iron Islands, in order to bring back pyrites. First he enlarged his furnace; then he carved a piece of wood in the form of a mold, in such a manner that his bars were almost fashioned by the cast. All that took him thirty nights.

To begin with, he installed on the ledge making a tour of the well, to either side of the squid's passage, two strong mobile brackets, solidly fixed to the wall, destined to support the grille; at the extremity, he fixed a pulley. He had also fabricated two strong ropes that, rolled over the feet of the brackets, and able, thanks to a slip knot placed in the middle to make the grille descent by unrolling. He had taken the measures scrupulously, with facility; the squid had not seemed disquieted by the work, which was almost all executed during their absence. At their entrance he counted them many times, and retained the certainty that there were exactly thirty-eight, twenty adults and eighteen of various sizes.

This is the fashion in which he constructed his grille, because it was necessary that it could be closed in very little time and it had to have a surface area of more than fifteen square meters. Every piece of the grille was a two-meter bar terminating at each end in a ring—or, rather, a hole. Each flat bar presented a cutting edge on either side. First he connected four bars between the two brackets by means of bolts in the form of split pegs, the two legs of which he bent back with a hammer. He had prepared lighted bars that he placed in the form of an X in each square of the chain, in order that the smallest squid could not escape.

When everything was prepared he proceeded with the assembly, realized in three nights. For more surety he had stuck—or, rather, wedged—pieces of wood in the interstices of the rocks on the ride of the Black Lake, and he had driven in pieces of iron to which he would attach ropes in such a fashion as to draw the grille from outside, in order to fix it to the wall of the well and resist the efforts of the squid if they tempted to pull it inside. That was improbable; he had calculated on the stupidity of the monsters.

Finally, on the hundred and seventy-fifth day of the third year, the grille was ready to be dropped. He poured a large quantity of oil on to the ropes in order that the slide would be frictionless, and he waited.

As if they were in haste to know the outcome of such labors, the monsters jostled one another as they reentered, and in that tumult Jean had some difficulty counting them. Finally, he judged that the count was complete. He waited for another hour in order to allow them to settle, and then seized the handles of the capstan and released the ropes; with a mathematical precision the grille descended and sank a good meter into the sand of the cavern; sliding along the wall, it sealed the entrance hermetically.

The squid did not seem to suspect anything; they did not budge. Jean emerged from the well, running along the crevice in spite of the heat of the day, reentered his dwelling and went as rapidly as possible to the place where he lodged his launch. He leapt into it, rowed around the volcano and penetrated into the Black Lake. The mass of the volcano shielded him from the sun and rendered the task less fatiguing.

Jean extended four sturdy ropes over the grille in order that it could not be forced from the interior. The squid were imprisoned. They had nothing more to do but devour one another or die of hunger.

This time, Jean was triumphant. It only remained to go home and have a well-earned meal. He leaned on the oars in order to return. He had only covered a few brasses when he heard a click behind him. The boat stopped dead. Jean turned round and was petrified momentarily. Instinctively, he threw himself toward the prow.

Two enormous tentacles palpated the launch and advanced almost as far as him. Almost immediately, the monster's head rose above the water and its enormous eyes fixed on him; then two more tentacles emerged from the sea and fell upon his body. Instinctively, he evaded one, but the other fell on a piece of amblyrhynchus leather that was protecting his shoulders and upper body from the sun, fixing itself there by means of it suckers.

The imminence of the peril finally rendered Jean the usage of his limbs and his thoughts. The other tentacle had fallen into the boat, coiling around the bench; that was what prevented him from being drawn immediately toward the atrocious beak, which opened in order to tear him apart. The animal made the same effort with both tentacles, drawing the boat and the man simultaneously.

Jean seized the knife hooked into his belt, and with a terrible thrust, cut through the hideous limb hanging on to his shoulder. He was free. He launched himself backwards at the moment when two more of the squid's tentacles sprang out of the sea in order to enlace him. He plunged his knife between the monster's two eyes, directly above the horrible beak.

The animal agitated in terrible convulsions, carrying away the launch like a wisp of straw. Jean was thrown into the sea and reached open water, swimming away as fast as possible from the site of the battle. Fortunately, the monster attacked the boat furiously. Gradually, however, its strength was ebbing away. A kind of black liquid flowed through its two wounds into the sea. In very little time the waves were tinted a beautiful sepia color.

Finally, the exhausted cephalopod ceased struggling; it died, remaining fixed desperately to the launch by the inextricable knots of its tentacles.

When Jean was quite sure that the monster was dead, he approached the launch, which, half-full of water, was threatening to sink. He hastened to cut the tentacles clinging to the boat, and the body of the squid sank to the bottom of the water. The launch lightened, Jean emptied it with the aid of his hat. He was fortunate enough to recover his oars, and this time, he reached Bon Repos.

In the evening, as soon as the sun had disappeared, he went to the central well to see what had become of his prisoners. They were agitating, because for them, it was time to leave. Already, three were before the grille, which they were palpating with their tentacles. They tried to shake it, but the flat and trenchant bars cut into their flesh and they were obliged to renounce it. Gradually, the others arrived, and there was a frightful swarming of tentacles, agitating and tangling like snakes, irritated by the unfamiliar obstacles. They were powerless against it. They entered into a rage and started fighting among themselves.

In that melee, Jean could not see anything clearly, but, drawn by the need to take an active part in the battle, he returned to Bon Repos, made a large sponge of coconut fiber, soaked it in oil, and then, carrying a lighted torch, he returned to the well. He attached his package to the grille and set fire to it. An immense sheaf of flames rose up, illuminating the entire gulf splendidly from the base to the summit.

Frightened, the monsters stopped fighting in order to plunge under water. Nevertheless, Jean had time to launch a dozen arrows that, being well-aimed, wounded or killed.

The improvised torch only lasted for a few minutes, being too rapidly extinguished; again, a demi-obscurity reigned over the abyss.

Now that he had fought one of the terrible monsters body to body they inspired less terror in Jean, so he resolved to return to the Black Lake in order to battle the prisoners through the grille. He was in haste to get rid of those terrible and repulsive neighbors forever. He therefore took his bow, fifty arrows, two long spears, his ax and his knife.

When he arrived at the grille, the moon, which was almost full, illuminated as if in the broad daylight of his native land the landscape of rocks and ocean with a magical light.

It seemed to him that the number of squid was already sensibly diminished. Some were dead, and the wounded were numerous. In their stupid struggle they were turning their rage against one another and tearing one another apart gladly. Jean augmented their anger and their disorder by piercing them with spear-thrusts and arrows.

Finally, the battle ended. The last survivors retired to the depths of the abyss and Jean returned to his lodgings with the certainty of being rid of the monsters forever.

He repeated the excursion for several nights. No squid presented itself at the grille. Prudently, he left it in place, contenting himself with taking back the ropes.

The hero had nothing more to fear from the tyrants of Harvez Island.

CHAPTER XXVII
Escape Attempt

Jean wanted to defend himself against the memory of Nano. The battle delivered and then won against the monsters had been a powerful distraction from his obsession. He wanted to try to leave, to quit the island, to try to forget—and, in sum, to rebuild his life ordinarily, among ordinary people.

He had confided to the ocean, a hundred and eighty days ago, his first document indicating his presence on the island. Since then he had thrown another. For almost six months, no one had responded to his appeal.

He wanted to make a supreme attempt, and he set about constructing a new apparatus to attract attention. He took it as far as possible out to sea. He recommenced that appeal three times. The result being negative, he would attempt to depart on a sort of raft attached to his launch. He knew what dangers awaited him, but he could not remain much longer in that tragic isolation.

Jean sometimes senses his brain capsizing; then he wants to escape, and he dreams about a normal, reasonable life; quitting the island where his statue, The Alluring, would sleep forever, while he, a creature of flesh, would love a creature of flesh. He would marry, he would have children, he would make sacrifices for them; he would have lives to guide, to sculpt marvelously; his sons and daughters would be beautiful and noble.

To leave, to leave! Jean no longer dreams about anything but leaving.

He has studied the velocity of the current that goes around the island. It is rapid and heads southwards. The seas of the southern hemisphere are much vaster than those of the northern hemisphere; thus, there is much less chance of the coconuts containing a message on a float being encountered. Now that material needs are tyrannizing Jean less, he is able to consecrate a considerable part of his nights to various tasks.

For example, he applied himself to augmenting his equipment and his vessels. In pottery he achieved marvelous results. He even obtained enamels of an unequaled color and brightness by adding metallic oxides found with the pyrites on the two Iron Islands.

Thinking about the current, Jean feared, if he headed directly southwards, reaching the polar regions, where everything carried in that direction would be lost in the ice. Finally, he made a decision. It would soon be three years that he had been here. If he were not rescued sooner, he would quit the island on the last day of the third year.

One evening, Jean departed in the launch, towing the floating apparatus bearing his call for help. He allowed himself to be carried beyond the limit of the visibility of the island, about forty kilometers.

Abruptly, the current became turbulent, and dragged him into a sort of spiral, rather similar to the Maelstrom, a gulf of the Arctic Ocean situated, as everyone knows, in the vicinity of the Lofoten Islands off the coast of Norway.

Here, the diameter of the whirlpool seemed far more extensive, very low on the waves. He was therefore drawn away without any means of resistance. After a dozen circuits he found himself at the center, where he thought he would be swallowed up. Nothing of the sort:

by virtue of a singular phenomenon, which he could not explain, the spiral of attraction was reversed and he was drawn outwards this time.

A few hours later he was floating in the current again. After the appearance of the sun, which had risen, it appeared to him that he had been deflected south-westwards. It was already twelve hours since Jean had quit the island. He set about trying to return. Not wanting to find himself in the whirlpool again, he rowed energetically to reach the limit of the current and to go alongside it as far as the vicinity of the island. That was a difficult task; the sun was rising higher and higher; fortunately, the sail, which was hoisted, gave a little shade.

The entire day passed in alternatives of toil and repose. Finally, night fell. Jean slept for three or four hours, and ate the rest of his provisions. He had had the good idea of bringing four nuts full of a mixture of water and coconut alcohol, obtained by fermentation and subsequent distillation. He still had one of those nuts; he kept it preciously in the bottom of the boat, under a sack, which he moistened continually in order to preserve it. He rationed it, anticipating that there would doubtless be a long delay before he returned home.

Without that foresight he would probably have succumbed. He only reached the limit of the current shortly before sunrise. He was just in time; he could do no more, suffering from fatigue and hunger. It was easy to maintain himself on that oceanic limit, sensibly darker than within the current. Was he far from the island? There could be no indication. It was probable that during the traversal of the current he had been dragged further away from it. Fortunately, a light breeze was blowing from the south; he orientated his sail as best he could, and then lay down in its shadow and went to sleep.

He changed place several times. The burning of the sun woke him up, but he went back to sleep immediately. The day went by like that. With the night, energy returned to him. He resumed rowing, taking care not to move far from the edge of the current.

The night went by. At sunrise he climbed up on the bench and looked northwards. Nothing was visible on the horizon. He began to despair, but by then he had endured so many proofs victoriously that he thought that, after having struggled for such a long time, it would be stupid to finish thus.

He spent the day, therefore, like the preceding one, forgetting his suffering in slumber. He had been asleep for a few hours when the agitation of the boat woke him up.

The sun had disappeared. The sky was a leaden gray. The sea began to rise in long, flat and viscous waves; a tempest was in preparation. He knew its violence by experience. He did not have time to make long reflections. An enormous wave came running from the north, driven by a terrible wind. It bounded over the little mast, which it tore away with a superhuman effort and threw into the sea, with the sail and the rapidly severed rigging.

At the same time, Jean felt himself lifted up. The wave had fallen a few meters from the launch, and then lifted it up from beneath like a wisp of straw, to throw it on to the crest of the following wave. It was as rapid as lightning—but he had had time to see his island on the horizon. The arrival of a sort of violent wind pushed the launch directly toward it. There was no possibility of struggle; Jean lay down in the prow, holding one of the oars in front of him, and waited. It collided suddenly with a rock, with such violence that he was lifted up and thrown into the sea, while the boat was smashed against the steep shore of an islet.

By swimming, he succeeded in reaching the shore, on to which he contrived to hoist himself. He covered a hundred meters at a run and slid into a fissure between two enormous rocks. He was scarcely sheltered than the rain began to fall in a downpour. He was able to drink until he was sated, which refreshed him somewhat. The rain was diluvian and the wind blowing so hard that he had to cling on in order not to be thrown back into the sea. Lightning flashed, thunderbolts falling continually, pulverizing the rocks, shards of which fell back around Jean. The entire gamut of horrors passed over him that he had been able to avoid thus far, in the shelter of Bon Repos.

By the incessant glare of the lightning, taking advantage of every petty calm, he succeeded in reaching a little grotto that he knew. There he stayed, protected against the wind and the rain, for it was necessary not to think of crossing the strait. He could only do that the next day, when the tempest had ended.

A few hours later, he was at home, where he had a meal and obtained some restorative sleep. Once again, Jean had escaped death.

The latest danger he had run was not useless. It had given him some precious information regarding the nature of the great current that went around the island.

Thus, he found himself increasingly isolated. The whirlpool, which he had escaped so miraculously, constituted one danger more for ships that attempted to approach the island on the side not surrounded by reefs.

And he returned, not immediately, to see his gigantic Idol, which nature had made and his art had completed. One might have thought that the feminine statue, which drew him with the memory of her sex—further affirmed by the triangular sign of the fingers before her lap—was reclaiming her prey.

CHAPTER XXVIII
The Alluring

He did everything possible to forget Nano. He devoted himself to his habitual work of renewing his food supplies, attempted a few ameliorations in his habitation and his clothing.

One morning, he woke up greatly inconvenienced by a singular odor. It was coming from the tunnel at the back, formed by an amalgam of putrid and musky gases. It was still tolerable, but would become insipid before long.

Jean, never stopped by vain hesitations, equipped himself with several candles and went into the tunnel to see what it was.

Having arrived at the central well he attached several torches together, lit them and lowered them into the well, where a complete obscurity reigned. That astonished him, for normally, some light always came in through the opening to the sea. He let out the rope, much more than should have been required to reach the surface of the water.

He had almost reached the end of his coil when the improvised chandelier touched the bottom. Its light, although enfeebled by distance, allowed Jean to observe that the bottom of the well was dry; around the luminous circle, beautiful yellow sand extended, stained here and there with black.

He understood that the cadavers of the squid were producing the odor. How had it come about that the well was dry? He withdrew his improvised chandelier, examining the walls of the well. At the location of the natural porch that allowed sea water in, the grille was still in place, but the opening was blocked. Doubtless there had been an external landslide. By swinging his light-source around in all directions, Jean remarked below him a kind of fissure in the wall of the well, which descended at a sufficiently gentle slope all the way to the bottom of the abyss. The descent did not seem to be impossible.

That fissure was three or four meters below him. With one of his ropes he would be able to risk it.

While he was making that observation, time had passed and sunrise was imminent. Jean was getting ready to return to Bon Repos when the well was suddenly illuminated brightly.

Then, everything was explained to him; the side of the central cone facing the sea had crumbled; the mass of debris had blocked the entrance employed by the squid. Thus, the latter would have been consecrated to certain death anyway, unless they had been outside when the catastrophe occurred.

In the meantime, the central cone was destroyed to a height of at least a hundred meters. Through that opening, light illuminated the abyss almost all the way to the bottom. He could see quite distinctly the black patches of the cadavers cutting across the brighter color of the sand.

That catastrophe must have occurred during his absence, in the latest tempest. It was certain that he would have heard the din of the collapse had he been at home.

Suddenly, a cold sweat moistened his temples. That catastrophe might perhaps have had a repercussion in the Well of Light…and on the statue?

He launched himself forth like a madman, returned to Bon Repos, climbed the ladder, and reached the great chamber in a matter of minutes.

Nothing. The colossal Lover and her desirous adorer loomed up, both superb in their impeccable nudity, in the eternal silence.

With the same crazed precipitation, Jean fled to Bon Repos. He threw himself down on his bed and sobbed desperately, like a child.

CHAPTER XXIX
The Well of the Squid

That same evening he made a tour of the central cone to see what new appearance the Black Lake had. It was a long journey. No longer having his boat, he was obliged to go on foot via the northern landslides. Nevertheless, the route was more aerated that usual. The disturbance caused by the collapse of that part of the central cone had caused a kind of aggregation of the entire neighboring region. The landslides had experienced it in particular.

Having gone around the rocky cone, Jean was amazed by the change produced in that location.

The Black Lake still existed, but reduced in dimension by half. The central cone had been eviscerated all the way to the cliffs. One could see in full illumination the interior of the volcano, the vitrified walls of which were sparkling under the lunar radiation with a thousand changing reflections. At the base, the collapses had created a kind of causeway that would henceforth permit a complete circuit. Under the formidable shock, a large section of the cliffs had crumbled, and enormous masses of rock were strewing the ground.

Henceforth, Jean would have much easier access to the Black Lake. He climbed over the landslides as far as the rip without too much difficulty and darted a glance into the interior of the volcano. The aspect was similar to the view from inside, but from here he saw that he could reach the fault without needing rope. He attempted that dangerous route with the skill of a chamois-hunter.

In a matter of minutes he reached the bottom of the well. The stink of the rotting squid was less perceptible down there. He examined the walls of the central well attentively. In various places, the calcined or vitrified parts had flaked away under the action of the water, allowing the primitive rock to be seen. Softer than the granite, it had allowed itself to be attacked by sea water, hollowing out numerous caverns there.

In the hope of making a few interesting discoveries, he scratched the walls with his knife, detached large fragments of marine salt. He had never lacked salt; he found it easily at the edge of the sea, but he had never had crystals of this size.

On closer examination she saw gilded particles shining. He dug into the sand at the base of one of the fissures, plunged his hand into it and brought a fistful to the surface, Specks of gold glittered in quantity. He heaped up ten kilos in a sack and climbed the escarpment again.

He reached Bon Repos well before sunrise. Hs first concern was to fetch a few receptacles in order to wash the sand. It contained at least twenty per cent gold by weight, so that he had at least five hundred grams.

Given the diameter of the central well and the fantastic quantity of gold-bearing sand that it contained, there was wealth there sufficient to cause vertigo. Jean had become the possessor of a fortune that could buy the world. A first, he was bewildered by it; then reason returned, and he understood the utter futility of such a discovery.

He had thought, for the conservation of the statue of the woman of diverting the course of the siliceous spring so that it would not thicken the pure lines of the Alluring over time. Why, now, should he not cover it with a layer of gold that would render it unalterable forever?

It was necessary, at any price, to find means to occupy his mind and his body. Jean strove to regain his empire. He felt, bitterly, that it was necessary for him to work on some project. But his brain, empty of desires, sometimes left him inert and impotent.

He began spending his days between the sand, amassed in large sacks, and then washed in order to extract the gold, and a contemplative abandonment in confrontation with the statues.

What was the point of protecting Nano? Who would ever see her? No ship would ever reach the island; it would break up on its inhospitable shores.

Jean lost the bright and pure joy of the artist, which had rendered him equal to God. Things created and to be created left him indifferent from day to day.

He experienced the sensation of being nothing but an irresponsible atom, a tiny body tossed hither and yon, on which a sentence of death had been passed. Why squander the hours in vain and sterile struggles?

No matter! He protested; since the statue was finished, he would divert the petrifying spring.

And he would gild the statue.

That new project was a further distraction from his isolation. But when that result was obtained, what would he do?

In the depths of human being, smallness engenders grandeur, and the voluptuous spasm of an isolated individual still creates beauty, in spite of everything.

He now had close at hand, gilded and monumental, Nano, Nini, the adoring, his "niña." What more was he waiting for?

He was no longer, in fact, waiting for anything. He remained lying down for entire days, motionless, staring at the magical lake were two naked reflections joined one another and were married, that of the man and that of the woman.

His body weakened, his mind was inflamed by thoughts that were increasingly troubled. They soon engendered delirium. The grotto resounded with Jean's voice, full of appeals, cries of terror and dolorous laughter.

He saw the ship sinking…his incessant struggles…the embrace of the squid…the stinking cadavers at the bottom of the grotto…and above all that, the discovered gold, the flecks of gold, the molten gold, flowing marvelously over the naked feminine idol, covering everything.

Jean sometimes threw himself upon the statue, The Alluring, digging his fingernails, almost claws, into the stone at the point of attack.

One day, having bounded upon her more furiously, his head collided with the smooth belly. Something near the navel cracked against the wall of his skull; blood trickled, mingled with the gray matter of the brain.

He collapsed, struck forever, imploring her, appealing to her, as if she were giving herself to him, in the lap of the troubling and monumental statue: The Alluring.

His arms clinging to the loins of his amour, of his work, Nano, of his mistress, his body stuck to the entrance to her vagina, he had the impression of possessing her eternally, without being able to die, in bewildered death-throes, in which the desire of a virile artist, deprived for three years of any human contact, cried out.

CHAPTER XXXI
The Disappearance of a Volcanic Island

On 8 December 1922 there was an extraordinary meeting of the Academy of Sciences of Rio de Janeiro. The hall was full. A convocation had been addressed to all the foreign members. The reason was so uncommon that they had all responded to the summons.

On 22 April of the previous year, the yacht of the multimillionaire Fairpoint, returning from a cruise in the southern polar regions, had found, engaged in the channel of a plain of ice, through which it was fraying a passage with difficulty, a bizarre floating apparatus bearing in its center a box covered in an unalterable varnish. The opened box, yielded a document. It was the appeal for help of a victim of the shipwreck of the transatlantic liner *España*, torpedoed in 1915 by the Germans. The signatory, a sculptor famous in Brazil, known above all for a marvelous work, The Alluring, had quit Brazil in order to go and offer to France the assistance of his humanity. The sculptor had been carried by a current of water to a volcanic island in the tropical region. He gave a few indications in the hope of being rescued. That document was transmitted by Sir Arthur Fairpoint to the government in Rio; the latter immediately decided to send a scientific commission to search for the island and bring back the castaway to his homeland. Very interested by that strange adventure, Mr. Fairpoint offered his yacht to transport the commission, which left Rio on 17 June 1921.

There was no news for almost fifteen months.

Finally, on 19 November, the commissioned signaled its return, after having discovered Harvez Island. Public opinion was impassioned by that sensational adventure; the world press, in its entirety, associated its curiosity. But the yacht did not bring back the castaway. After an initial report to the Brazilian government an official communication was issued.

The secretary of the Academy stood up in the midst of a profound silence:

"Messieurs,

"If ever fatality, the chopping-bock of many human endeavors has revealed itself with its implacable cruelty, it is in the events that I am about to narrate to you. The commission sent to search for our glorious but unfortunate compatriot, the sculptor of genius Jean Harvez, after months of research, finally found the current identified by the castaway: a fatal current in which they nearly perished.

"There is a whirlpool in mid-ocean, with a radius of rotation of nearly ten kilometers. If our explorers had arrived in that region in bad weather, they would have been doomed. Fortunately, they were sailing then, to use the corsair expression, on a seal of oil. They succeeded, thanks to the skill of Captain John Harrison, in passing through. The next day, the island, a volcanic terrain previously unknown, came in sight. The opinion of Captain Harrison and the members of the scientific commission is that the ignorance of that island was due to the terrible current, in which all those who engaged in it must have perished.

"The island was the effect of a sudden upheaval followed by several volcanic eruptions. Like all islands surrounded by shallow waters it was in the process of growing by virtue of the formation of coral reefs, surrounding it almost entirely."

At this point, a projection showed a map of the island, carefully drawn up by the commission. The orator described the configuration and then resumed.

"Who would have believed that in such a desolate abode, a human being could live and struggle victoriously against terrible monsters and the hostile elements? Life in the sunlight is impossible there! However, against that impossibility, a man, a Brazilian, struggled.

"The commission followed, so to speak, all his deeds and actions. It discovered his dwelling, a cavern situated *here*"—he pointed at the map—"at the entrance to this singular defile, the overflow of an artificial river.

"That man, having arrived naked on an island of stone and sand, was able to supply all his needs and, as you will see, to undertake works of a very elevated order.

"The explorers discovered in a cavern a statue of a woman, about five meters high, so beautiful and pure that at first, the commission could only look at it ecstatically. It was like a replica of Harvez's masterpiece, The Alluring, but how superior! Here, on this screen, are photographs; judge for yourselves."

Images of the idol appeared. An admiring murmur ran through the assembly.

The voice of the secretary rose up again, slow and solemn.

"Subjugated by the admirable masterpiece, you only see that. There is, however, something else. At the foot of the grandiose work, nested in her lap, lies a skeleton with white bones, curled up. That is the artist, whose flesh has been eaten there by crabs."

A long silence followed these words.

The projection now presented a man standing on a siliceous block, marvelous in strength.

"Facing the statue, however, Jean Harvez has sculpted his own body in a pose typical of Eros. We cannot, without being profoundly moved, see here the complete, and excessively free, image of our friend.

"The commission wanted to bring back these masterpieces immediately. Some members wanted to leave them in the frame that their creator had intended for them.

"Nature provided the response.

"Scarcely had the ship reached the open sea in order to return to Rio, to prepare another expedition, than a spray of flame sprang forth over the ocean, amid thunderclaps.

"The volcano was erupting. The yacht only just had time to escape the small, sinister and rapid earthquake.

"Messieurs, The Alluring, Jean Harvez and their island, presently engulfed, no longer exist."

Paris, 1931.

ALSO FROM BLACK COAT PRESS

www.ingramcontent.com/pod-product-compliance
Lightning Source LLC
Chambersburg PA
CBHW032148020726

47496CB00003B/776

* 9 7 8 1 6 1 2 2 7 9 0 9 1 *